Praise for
The Act of Contrition

More than just about any other writer I can think of, Joseph Bathanti's work has always felt like life to me. Perhaps it resonates with my own life—regional identity, blue collar background—or perhaps it resonates with the many mysteries of the lives of others that I often find myself wondering about. Bathanti does what the best realists do: he brings beauty to the terror of the mundane, mystery to the overlooked desperation of people we might never meet in real life but will know intimately because we have met them in Bathanti's fiction. The stories in this collection continue a long career that has found Bathanti plumbing the depths of the human heart and untangling mystery all the while.

—Wiley Cash, author of
When Ghosts Come Home

Joseph Bathanti's [illegible]'s is a beautiful bo[illegible] passionate and bol[illegible]g, that recreates in rich de[illegible] life, a culture, a community, and the deepest struggles of its wonderfully evoked characters.

—Phil Klay, author of
Redeployment

Joseph Bathanti's stories thrilled and enchanted me. His capacity to create truly memorable characters, deeply rooted in time and place—in this case Pittsburgh in the fifties, sixties and seventies—is fueled by a fiercely unsentimental love that imbues every story. His writing, line by line, is consistently brilliant, without ever losing touch with the highly textured Italian and Irish blue-collar worlds where his characters struggle. Bathanti has given us stories that never shy away from life's heartbreaks, while also offering us the protection of his compassionate insights, his humor, and the spirit of love that shines so vividly throughout this book.

—Jane McCafferty, author of
Director of the World and Other Stories

In story after story, we find ourselves in the hands of a writer who writes solid, elegant sentences, and who takes us into the lives of his characters to reveal the way the extraordinary is so often realized in the seemingly ordinary. Take your time and savor this beautifully written and often surprising collection of stories.

—Silas House, author of
Southernmost

The Act of Contrition & Other Stories

*

JOSEPH BATHANTI

THE ACT OF CONTRITION & OTHER STORIES
Joseph Bathanti

FICTION
ISBN 978-1-958094-27-3

BOOK DESIGN ⁕ EK Larken
COVER DESIGN ⁕ Margaret Yapp

Cover image courtesy of author's personal collection.
Author photo by David Silver.

Grateful acknowledgment is extended to the following journals in which some of these stories, in some cases different versions, first appeared: "Infestation" in *The Florida Review;* "The Pall Bearer" in *Hotel Amerika;* "The Gazebo" in *Kestrel;* "The Act of Contrition" in *Louisiana Literature;* "Acid" in *Northern Appalachian Review;* "A Story of Glass" in *Paterson Literary Review;* "Rita's Dream" in *Shenandoah;* "Hosanna," "My Only Crack at Beauty," and "The Malocchio" in *South Dakota Review;* "Buon Anno" in *Upstreet;* "The Day John Wayne Died" in *Weber: The Contemporary West;* and "Claire as the Blessed Mother" in *You Are the River: Literary Expressions of the North Carolina Museum of Art.*
"Rita's Dream" won the 2014 Shenandoah Fiction Prize.

⁕

EastOver Press encourages the use of our publications in educational settings. For questions about educational discounts, contact us online:.
www.EastOverPress.com *or* info@EastOverPress.com

PUBLISHED IN THE UNITED STATES OF AMERICA BY

ROCHESTER, MASSACHUSETTS
www.EastOverPress.com

Contents

The Act of Contrition

& Other Stories

Fred

My parents found Fred sitting at a parking meter on Highland Avenue the morning they stormed out of Foxx's Grille after last call. Next to the expired meter, where their uninspected '61 beige Impala slouched, Fred clocked his last minutes of lost and hopeless, pondering suicide, perhaps praying for my mother, his queen, to appear in the snowstorm.

There was always a snowstorm with my mother – always life and death, nothing in between. Only the brink. Mysteriously overcome by Fred, she knelt in the slush, threw her arms around him, and drew his face to hers. Fred held her tightly, if that can be said of a dog.

My dad loved my mother, God help him, and he recognized the moment as a twist in their lives, a tableau he was moved by; but he also knew that trouble would likely follow, and he wanted to leave it there on the sidewalk – just a beautiful, inexplicable moment, the lamp of grace flickering for a few seconds.

When they strolled just a couple doors down the avenue to Vento's, Fred followed and stared through the glass storefront as they ate pizza at the counter. When they left Vento's, they sat on the curb and petted Fred. My mother kissed him. She fed him pepperoni from the to-go slices meant for me. She confessed to my father that she wanted to keep this dog.

Very gently, my father explained the complications of taking the dog home to our small duplex on Saint

Marie Street. They worked nights at restaurant jobs, slept most of the day. They liked to go out for drinks after their shifts and lead the nocturnal life. I was just a freshman in high school, gone most of the day myself. Dogs need attention. Fred was pretty banged up. He'd have to be checked out by a vet. He'd need dog food, a collar, and leash. They knew nothing about him – his pedigree and temperament, where he came from, his secrets and desires, if he could be trusted. My father went as far as he thought prudent without riling my mother. Flakes of silver snow lit in her yellow hair.

My dad didn't drive, and my mother had had too much to drink. They never bothered with snow tires or chains. So, the three of them – Fred, my mother's arm around him, as she drove left-handed, hunkered in the front seat between my parents – skidded the half-mile or so to Saint Marie. When they got home, at 2:30, early for them, they woke me, and there was Fred – of suspect ancestry, one of those refugee mutts that suddenly showed up in East Liberty, scrounged nomadically through the streets and alleys like a junkie, then split. He sat next to my bed, gazing contemplatively at me, like we knew each other: desperate, dark brown eyes – like my mother's – matted chestnut coat; snowy diamond blaze at his throat; bushy, black-tipped tail clotted with filth; a chewed-up ear; an eye with a gash above it. A little gaunt for a welterweight, but good-looking and athletic – cagey. He'd come of age on the streets. He knew what was what.

My mother swore he was a collie. Each time she said this, my father's blue, Black Irish eyes registered skepticism. Otherwise, he remained impassive and, when pressed, agreed with her: *Fred was a collie.* What kind of dog Fred was didn't matter. He made my mother happy. I hadn't even known she liked dogs. My dad was easy with dogs, as he was with everything, but he didn't want another living thing beyond my mother and me to worry about.

It was mid-February – I was thirteen – the last weeks of wrestling season. I'd been pinned in the tournament just two days before, and I hated myself. My season was finished. My dad told me he was proud of me for going out for the team, that I had nothing to reproach myself over. He knew from experience that you did not have to join a wrestling team to get your ass kicked. No need to go looking for it. My mother, too, knew all about ass-kickings. She felt badly that I had lost and been humiliated. But she was mad at me for losing, as if a stranger had laid on top of her, instead of me, and pressed her to the stinking rubber mat until the ref's palm clapped off it like a backhand across the face.

I wasn't a very good wrestler. I'd never go out again. Nothing but gristle, pared to the bone, from weeks and weeks of starving myself to make weight, I had sat, during the season, in the cafeteria at Saint Sebastian's eating lettuce and honey as fourteen hundred boys devoured their ample lunches, then bought Ho Hos and Twinkies, ice cream sandwiches and candy bars from the vending machines. I dwindled, became invisible, silent. I could not tolerate an unkind word.

I still had the shakes and a bird-like, twitching vigilance. My eyes stood out from my head, my cheeks and flanks sunken – and so was I. But I lied to my mother when she exacted from me the promise that I'd train for the next season and kick the shit out of anyone who got in my way. Wrestling is a sport when, even if you win, you get your head handed to you.

My mother had already named the stray: Fred, from *Federico*, her father's name – Federico Schiaretta, a shoemaker who had died when his shop inexplicably took fire before I was born, when my mother was a girl of nine. Like Fred the dog, I had also been named for my grandfather. My mother had insisted upon this. My father, who had known my grandfather and refrained from commenting on him, had not raised a fuss. I don't know what name my father would have chosen for me; he subscribed to *What's in a name?* At any rate, he played along, and they named me Frederick, even though at home I was called Fritz. and my friends called me Sweeney, our last name, which I preferred. My father's name was Travis, an English name that means *crossing* or *crossroads*. All the other dads in the neighborhood were Joe and Mike and Tony. My mother's name was Rita, from Carita. It means *beloved*. It means *charity*.

But Fred, the dog, could not be blamed for anything. Abandoned, the product of some Booze Alley tryst between heathen mongrels, he was on the lam, a constant eye out for the dog catcher and the vault bolted to the back of his truck where the likes of Fred were gassed. He was a poor-mouth dog – not a pot to piss in – terrified of what terrifies us all: being put to sleep. Yet, now he was ours, and there was that novel thrill that I had never known – the first moments of a new dog in the house. As he did my mother, Fred made me happy. I had never had a dog.

My parents turned off my bedroom light. I had to be up for school in four hours. My mother escorted Fred to the bathroom. I drifted off to the sound of water splashing into the bathtub and my mother cooing: *Fred was a good boy, the best boy. She loved him and would take care of him always. He now belonged to us. Forever.*

When I went down for cereal the next morning, Fred was in the kitchen, barricaded behind a rampart rigged from the hassock and ironing board. He smelled like my mother. She had sprayed him with Chantilly after his bath. Stretched on the linoleum, he eyed me soulfully. He looked like a million bucks after his bath and a few good hours of sleep in a warm, safe place: his fluffy shimmering coat was like a new suit of clothes; the cut over his eye was barely visible; his ear looked better. Scattered across the floor were remnants of my lunch – a couple of baggies, a banana peel, an apple core, scraps of the brown paper bag with my name scrawled across it. My dad had it stationed every morning on the kitchen table, two quarters beside it. When he actually packed it, I never knew.

Fair enough: who knew when Fred had last eaten. I cleaned up the mess, tied my bathrobe belt around his neck and led him outside. Ten degrees, if the old, rusted, Town Talk Bread thermometer dangling from the back stoop could be trusted. Another six inches of snow on top of what had been there all winter. In my slippers, I trudged Fred through the drifts until he peed – a long cursive sentence I couldn't quite decipher, golden against the blinding white. I went back inside, grabbed a can of Campbell's soup from a cabinet, and bashed a hole in the ice coating the surface of my little blue plastic swimming pool, flopped in the yard since my parents first bought it for me when I was four. Fred dipped his face into the jagged opening and drank for a long time. Before I caught my bus for school, we each had a bowl of cereal, I put out water for him and I packed another lunch. My parents would not stir for another six or seven hours.

I was blue about losing so badly, so publicly, in the tournament. Tragically pinned in what seemed mere seconds in my inaugural match of the tournament. My soul jackknifed out of me in front of a thousand strangers, in a colossal Catholic gymnasium, by another boy exactly my weight, down to the ounce, a boy much better than I, the boy I had the chance to be, but not the gumption – his breath, his hands on me. *The Daily Bulletin* broadcasted over the PA to all the home rooms the names of the Saint Sebastian wrestlers who had moved ahead in the tournament. Everyone knew what had happened to me. But nobody said anything. Silence is not the same as respect, but it's often all we have. Why willingly take on another's pain? In truth, what is there to say, ever, really? My parents had said all they were equipped to say on the matter of my loss. They would probably be gone by the time I got home – not unusual, the house empty – but Fred would be there in the kitchen, as the late afternoon light quailed.

When I got home from school, a bag of dog food, a red leash, and collar lay in the kitchen, but no Fred. He'd busted out of his makeshift pen and was upstairs in my parents' bed, chewing on my mother's black sleep mask. The ashtrays on their nightstands were overturned, a lamp knocked over, a pile of shit beside the bed. He'd eaten their cigarettes. He looked strong, confident. I said, "What are you doing, Fred? My mother is going to kill you." He seemed to smile – *No, she's not.* And he was right. My mother thought the mangled sleep mask and gobbled cigarettes were funny – I had tidied everything up – and, after that, my parents simply closed their bedroom door when they departed for work every afternoon.

Fred began sleeping with Travis and Rita, in their bed, and, when I passed their open door after waking, he bounded from between them and followed me downstairs, where I leashed him and walked him through the snow, then loaded his bowl with dog food and replenished his water. He sat with me as I ate my cereal. I petted him and talked to him, and often he raised a paw and placed it on my thigh. He and I had the same name and were forced to share what, at the time, seemed my mother's limited store of love, though she seemed to prefer Fred over me and my father. When she was home, Fred was cuddled in her lap or at her feet, sometimes wrapped in a pink blanket. He followed her everywhere. She kissed and made over him the way one would a child, an infant. Baby talk. Songs. She heated cans of chicken noodle soup and poured it over his dog food.

He was her *baby*, her *good boy*, her *best boy*. She kept him bathed and powdered and perfumed, bought him toys and special bone-shaped dog treats, one end of which she held between her lips until Fred took it into his mouth. She also taught him a signature trick. He would sit motionless before her for several minutes. He was not permitted to move; he obeyed her perfectly. After what seemed like forever, she made her hand a pistol, put it between his eyes, and exclaimed: *Pow!* Fred collapsed as if a bullet had plowed through his cortex and lay still on the floor until my mother, like Jesus restoring Lazarus, finally called him back to life, then rewarded him with kisses and another dog treat. She also taught him to fetch her Chesterfields and Zippo. My father regarded these things with bemused forbearance, wondering when the inevitable shit would hit the fan – as it always did, like a thief in the night, with my mother.

My father was fed up with Fred, not because he didn't like him, and not because of his belief that dogs should not sleep in beds with people – which he tolerated to placate my mother – but because he saw my mother's infatuation with Fred as an attempt on her part to articulate something she could never forge into words – or simply refused to. My mother was always on the verge of slipping away, through that waiting trapdoor that capriciously opened and swallowed her – often for weeks at a time when she would walk silently, like a sleepwalker, past my father and me, refusing to speak or look at us, as if we were invisible. I didn't understand these spells, but their onset was palpable – a sky gradually blackening, her pensive stares and mutters as she lit Chesterfield after Chesterfield and sipped VO. I had felt it brewing in the days leading up to Fred. She was working herself up to something. For a long time, my mother had wanted to have another baby, but things hadn't worked out. So maybe Fred was that other baby – my brother. But he was also my grandfather. He was also me.

In religion class, we had studied reincarnation, which Catholics, strictly speaking, don't believe in, though it was never clear to me that my parents paid any attention to Catholic dogma. My mother prayed, but only out of desperation and superstition. She was waiting for something that did not exist in the flesh-and-blood world to rescue her. At his most religious, my father was agnostic – and made no bones about it. But at heart he was an atheist – something that troubled me. What he believed in more than anything was karma. Perhaps Fred was the reincarnation of my grandfather, Federico; the soul of a departed person could find new life in an animal's body. Fred's eyes were so much like my mother's, like mine, and my elusive namesake's eyes – Federico. I'd seen the photographs. My dad's eyes were blue with unsettling conviction, deep enough to drown in.

My father was simply biding his time – when to tell my mother that Fred either had to go or be treated more like a dog, but the stakes were precariously high, as they always were with her. Her likely comeback would be to tell my father that if anyone was leaving, it was him. He could get the hell out. He could go to hell. The dog was already sleeping in their bed. He had the same name as my father's son, and my father's wife's father. My dad had already mulled over this equation and its crazy Freudian implications, East Liberty style.

We had read *Oedipus Tyrannus* in freshman English. I loved it, especially when Oedipus jabs his eyes out with his mom's jewelry – so operatic, so Italian, something Rita Schiaretta Sweeney might do. "Look at me," she would hiss. "You see what you made me do. This is for you." Then – right through her pretty brown eyes, and my dad and I would be required to witness it. There might have been some kids in that class who wanted to murder their dads and marry their moms, but I was not one of them. What I learned, more than anything, in reading that play, was do not fuck with the gods. Fate terrified me.

Fred had been with us two weeks, a foundling plucked from the cold-hearted mayhem of the streets and given a home: food, warmth, and the devotion of a fiery, dyed-blond Napolitano woman who had fallen in love with him, and the feeling was clearly mutual. He slept between her and her husband every night and had a whole house to roam until she made it home with a half-pound of pastrami and boozy, maudlin kisses for him. My father and I treated Fred with unabashed affection and respect. We petted him and told him he was a good boy.

I spent more time with him than anyone. Fred and I sat side by side on the couch as I did homework. Together, we watched *The Mod Squad*, *The Beverly Hillbillies*, *My Three Sons*, and *Bewitched*. I loved having his company those winter nights when by five it was recklessly dark, my parents gone until nearly dawn, the dinner my father had fixed me, which I shared with Fred, stacked in the oven in aluminum foil. Our Christmas tree was still up, but that wasn't unusual. My dad said it was a Dutch tradition not to remove it until Easter, and my mother didn't care one way or another. It was a rickety little thing my dad had scored at Nicky D's car lot, by then drained of sap and haggard, most of the needles scattered over the garish creche, Baby Jesus smiling inanely in His diaper, a couple dozen red, blue, and green bulbs, candy canes and tinsel and colored lights I plugged in any time I was alone. But when I headed for bed, Fred refused to follow – he could have slept with me – but instead he stretched plaintively at the door and waited for my mother to blow in with the wind and snow and shoot him dead.

If Fred was working the system, who could blame him? We're all mutts that depend on the kindness of strangers: bumming smokes and change, sipping poorboys of homebrew with fellow sufferers in shivering East Liberty dead ends. Handouts, the dole, copping at the relief office. Dogs bloated in the weeds down The Hollow, a chorus of flies hovering split bellies. People threw pans of boiling water from second stories on strays who begged beneath their windows.

We didn't begrudge Fred a little happiness. He'd been fleeced, suckered, and bullied. He knew what it was like to be pinned, to have something vile hold you down and blow its rank breath down your throat – to shake hands with your executioner and make the mistake of looking into his eyes, and suddenly you're on your back, hallucinating, staring at the empty sky.

During those long nights in front of the colossal Magnavox, Fred and I wrestled. He weighed maybe forty pounds, still stringy from his days in the gutter, but filling out, the patches in his coat restored, lustrous. It was impossible to judge his age. We hadn't taken him to a vet. He was still young, roughly two years old, which in dog years put him and me at about the same age.

He was a wily wrestler, all feints and misdirection. He didn't muscle, refused to lock up, but pranced and dipped, jockeyed for the opening, and slipped in. He had gotten by with his good looks and wit, not his fists. He never nipped nor was unfair, and we always let it go at a draw. He might have even been taking it easy with me, holding back, sensing my own hard-luck story – as if he wanted me to win. We'd spar a bit, then ice cream and Carol Burnett.

But wresting season was over. I was attempting to get over that boy – though I never would – who had held me down against my will. I tried not to think about him. I tried not to think of what might lie ahead, not even the next day. Since the tournament, I no longer cared about what other people cared about. I pretended to care – even in front of my parents, who themselves cared for nothing others cared for. They were good people, but they had endured their families and their ancestries, as we all must, and the times in which they had lived: the silence and hysteria; the gothic secrets; East Liberty as poor kids during the Depression, then the war. Fate had insisted they meet, and things instantly detonated. They had had me the way you fall down the steps and crack your head open. When my mother – who was not a hitter, but a screamer – was mad at me, she would sometimes threaten, "I'll fracture your skull; I'll break both your legs."

With my season over, I had for company not only Fred, but suddenly the luxurious solace of food, which I had dreamt of every feverish night alone – my parents hours from finally waltzing back home. I could now eat anything at all. I imagined becoming obscenely overweight, blowing up, five-six hundred pounds, vicious as

Iggy, the mute gargantuan neighborhood savant who despised children and occasionally mangled one who strayed too close while taunting him. Like Iggy, I'd wear the same shit-brindle-brown suit, shirt and tie every day, join the cast of mythological East Liberty *mostros*. I'd been invisible so long, however; I wanted to stay that way. Iggy was such an exaggeration, so immense, so grotesque – the object of fear and scorn and laughter – he was unable to hide. Maybe someday I'd want to be seen again; but, for then, I just wanted to disappear.

Fred was of a similar maudlin, slightly tortured, romantic strain. Out there in the streets, on his own, homeless for so long – gaunt, starving, scuffed up, wary, and angry. Other dogs had abused him; people had thrown bricks and screamed filthy names at him. He'd fought when he could, but, like me, he wasn't a fighter and had done some things to survive that would always haunt him, lived through and witnessed some grave shit he simply wasn't up to talking about – worms and parasites, lapping up vermin and brackish water, abandoning dead comrades to the gutter. Dogs get punked, too. To further complicate things, he'd fallen in love with my mother.

Where had Fred come from? Who the hell was he? I asked him often when he and I were alone about his secret life before our house. He always seemed about to speak, really speak. His face a few inches from mine, his beautiful brown eyes bored deeply into my eyes as if he loved me in indescribable ways. Those dark cold nights when I could not fall asleep, and it was midnight, school the next morning, my parents still a few hours from punching out, and then whatever whim they struck up to amuse themselves – which didn't include coming home – I was sure I loved him, too, that I could trust him. But he had too much street in him, and those mysterious two years before that night on Highland Avenue in front of Foxx's. Like those kids who return from Juvenile Court or a stretch with the deranged Sisters of Divine Providence at Saint Joseph's Military School, or the first wave of draftees trickling back to East Liberty from Vietnam – they never really come back. Who knows? Maybe Fred didn't like answering questions. He was trying to start over. The past was past. Silence is often the only remaining dignity.

One night, while we wrestled, Fred growled and bit me, I'm certain by accident, maybe – not hard or enough to break the skin, but enough to let me know that he could kick my ass any time he felt like it – and it infuriated me. I wanted his real name. I wanted his story. I wanted the truth. Suddenly I didn't trust him – like those sky-high, scum-bag slickers down on Chookie's corner, mainlining and peddling dope and hot nylons and cigarettes and cameras out of their car trunks. Maybe we needed to check between the mattresses to make sure Fred hadn't fingered my parents' rainy-day stash or my mom's jewelry box.

I jumped from the floor, sank onto the couch, and screamed: "Who are you?"

Fred started violently, like he'd been shaken from a dream, glared at me, pupils dilated, then just the whites of his eyes, ears flattened, tail tucked. He shuddered, as if flashing back, slipping away, pinned down, bloodied, in a blind alley. There issued from him, though it seemed beyond the living room, beyond the house, a keening. He bared his teeth and whined. I scanned the room for something to smash him with if he lunged, but I was afraid to move, to breathe. I palpably reckoned his fear. The room vibrated with it. Not meanness nor ferocity, but abject terror. I knew not to make eye contact. I stared at the TV, so late it was just a white scrim of jagged crackling. Then Fred snapped out of it. He was back in the living room, and so was I, on the couch, on Saint Marie Street, though still he trembled.

He sauntered over, gazed at me with his soulful brown eyes, and timidly placed his paw on my thigh. I roughly brushed it away. "Fuck you," I said, instantly sorry, and told Fred so. I whistled and clucked for him, but he had sidled away, tail limp, eyes baleful, astonished: *Why do you hurt me like this?* It could have been an act. Maybe he was trying to tell me something. Like all of us, he was just scared, just trying to fit in, make a score, make a difference. Each night, before going to bed, I would hold him a moment and tell him good night, what a good boy he was. But that night, we parted in silence.

My parents' lone day off was Sunday. They rose in the afternoon, lounged all day, watched TV, smoked cigarettes, and drank. My dad pored over every inch of the big Sunday *Pittsburgh Press*. I loved Sundays, the only day I had with them. During the week, I saw them, maybe, for just a few hours during the day, occasionally after school, and not at all during wrestling season, because I got home from practice after they had left for work, and I always went to bed way before they got home.

There was a sacred hush about the house on Sundays – a blessed exhaustion, the thrum and meanness of eating shit for a buck six days a week forgotten. Nothing, no one, could harm us. My mother stayed in her robe all day. The three of us played Gin, 500 Rum, Monopoly, Uncle Wiggly; or just loafed, watched football, ate in front of Ed Sullivan and *Walt Disney's Wonderful World of Color* whatever splendid dish my dad miraculously threw together, and closed out the day with *Bonanza*. Then I climbed up to bed. The next morning, I had to catch the 73 Highland in time for 7:30 Home Room at Saint Sebastian's, but not before my dawn ritual with Fred.

I still faithfully attended Mass at Saints Peter and Paul, our parish, on Larimer Avenue, every Sabbath. That habit, however, dropped off in the next months and disappeared altogether by the time I reached fourteen. But, on this particular frigid Sunday, I was still a believer. I tiptoed out of the house and headed for church. In the middle of Larimer Avenue, in front of the parish rectory, lay a puppy, clipped by a car. A thread of blood leaked from its mouth. A little black girl, in a yellow dress – no winter coat in the unspeakable cold – held the hands of her barely walking brother and sister. The three of them stood above the dying dog, its eyes open. I stared at the dog. Its blood inscribed the filthy slush.

Ten feet away, across the street from the church, slumped CiCi's store, a falling-down neighborhood joint where you could get penny candy, pop, milk, and bread, salami, cheese, and olives. Cici hadn't opened yet, but at the store's stone entry smoldered my grandfather, Federico, in ash-gray clothes and a fedora spouting flame. This was not the first time I'd seen his shade. When I was just a child, perhaps four of five, I had come across him at a family Decoration Day picnic at North Park. His apparition could perhaps be explained away as a dream, a nightmare, but I knew better. In East Liberty, the dead have a place among the living, and, occasionally, they appear, though they are not permitted to speak.

That day in North Park, I had taken my grandfather's smoking hand, and he led me across a creek, then we played in the sand until he had to depart. I had attempted to follow him, but the living may not follow the dead. I was lost the entire afternoon. My mother found me, but I refused to mention this visitation of her father – and there he was again on the slab into Cici's, and there was the dying dog and the children. When Mass concluded, I left the church. Blood smeared the street, and Cici's store was open.

Under a lone swaying lightbulb, suspended from a sixteen-foot tin ceiling engraved with angels, loomed Cici behind his altar: a huge glass counter, atop which presided a gargoyle-like brass National Cash register, vats of pickled eggs and immense kosher dills; and, inside the counter, visible, overflowed caskets of jawbreakers, Sugar Daddies, Sputniks, Tootsie Rolls, root beer barrels, Mike and Ikes, Mary Janes, Fireballs, Chum Gum, Bazooka, Necco Wafers, Jujubes.

Cici was a dead ringer for Jimmy Durante, everything about him exaggerated: the monolithic nose and mammoth ears, hands that dangled six inches from the white cuffs of his shirt, giant feet angling from his wool trousers. He wore a snap-brim fedora, as did all the old Italian men, but he folded the brim up, a flourish that rendered him comical, like a circus clown. He did not speak – though he heard perfectly every tiny thing – and his eyes were those of a kestrel. Some infamy had stripped him of utterance, yet he habitually whistled lavish *villanellas*.

Cici was an archetype – like Tiresias in *Oedipus Rex* – an ancient, tetched sage, tortured by his visions of the future or, in this case, the past – which he was forbidden to divulge. He knew precisely what had transpired in my grandfather's shop the day of the fire – the two of them had been *paesani* – and I was certain my mother and father knew, as well, what had happened. In East Liberty, we were left ultimately with speculation, theories – which led to falsehood, which begat mythology, then tales, and eventually the troth to silence that perpetuated the falsehood.

The store smelled of fresh loam; Parodis; the salty, sharp, pungent, wine-sopped musk of cheeses and mortadella suspended from the rafters; olive brine. There was also the palpable hush of the *spettri*, among them my grandfather.

Cici smiled – he knew who I was – spread his arms wide from his long body like the transverse beam of the cross and whistled in *Abbruseze* the equivalent of *What would you like?* – though he reckoned exactly my desires.

I returned Cici's smile. I was not afraid of him. I strangely loved him. I arranged on the counter, head-up, one tarnished penny, doomed Lincoln's profile in concert with Cici's. He whistled a single shrill note, reached beneath the counter, and snagged a pack of Chum Gum. Then he throttled the register. It stuttered and whirred. Its drawer zipped out; numbers leapt into the tally window. He dropped my penny in its drawer, took out two pennies, slapped them and the Chum Gum on the counter in front of me, whistled again and smiled.

It was a game we played, and I did not forsake my part. "I can't accept these, CiCi," I said, nudging the two pennies back at him.

He made a doleful face, mitered together his spade-like gray hands, as if in prayer, then separated them, palms up in supplication, whistled and smiled – as if about to say what a man who had not spoken in over a quarter-century might suddenly say.

I scooped up the pennies and gum. Cici bowed, smiled, his teeth pearly blue under that watery light, and whistled his heartbreaking rendition of *La Pastorella.*

"Thank you, Cici."

He bowed again. What had taken his tongue?

Departing Cici's, I reminded myself that, mere minutes before, I'd received the Eucharist, and responded *Amen* when palsied Father Guisina placed the host upon my tongue and rasped *Corpus Christi.* I was in a state of sanctifying grace, my immortal soul immaculate as the suddenly falling snow – an opportune time to get run over or fall through a manhole: I'd go straight to Heaven. Yet my place was on the mysterious, troubling earth – and I craved that life more than Heaven, knowing that such desire for the fallen world was itself blasphemy. It would be years before I knelt again at the altar rail and proffered my tongue to my Savior; in the interim, I would defame my soul with mortal sin.

When I walked through the front door after Mass, the big fat Sunday *Pittsburgh Press* – with the *Roto Magazine* and *Parade* and the lavish anthology of color funnies – had been massacred, strewn through the living room, chomped and soggy. I smelled sauce. Heavenly. It was much too early for my parents to be about, but there in the kitchen stood my mother in an apron over her nightgown, making *braciole*, pounding flank steak to tenderize it with a beautiful hammer I had never seen before. Its wooden handle was worn smooth, burnished by repeated caresses; its black iron head like a sounding porpoise, the business end blunt, like a pig snout, perfectly round, the circumference of a silver dollar. The butt end swooped into a fluke – for prying. In my mother's mouth was a lit Chesterfield. At her feet, Fred gnawed the sports page.

She looked up and smiled. "Put your eyes back in your head."

"What are you doing?"

"What does it look like I'm doing?"

My mother occasionally heated things and made toast, but the only other time I had seen her cook, she had set herself aflame with a grease fire and then ignited my father as he rescued her. My dad had always been the cook in the house – exclusively – a most accomplished cook. But he had once confided that my mother was an expert in the kitchen (I had thought he was kidding); she just refused to do it.

"I decided we needed a little Italian cuisine today in this *Americano* house. Don't forget, Fritz. You're a Schiaretta. More Schiaretta than Sweeney. Your father's a good cook, but he never learned to cook Italian. I think it's deliberate. He looks down on Italians. He thinks of us as greenhorn guineas."

We had always eaten Italian exclusively in restaurants or take-out. My dad's specialties were meatloaf, pot roast, omelets. He could fix Welsh rarebit, scalloped potatoes, sauerkraut, leg of lamb, macaroni and cheese, any kind of soup, great fried chicken. He could whip up a cake or pie, cookies. But no Italian. Never.

This snipe at my father might've been harmless banter or a worrisome rough draft of the script she would try out on him when he eventually shuffled into the kitchen, groggy with sleep, and reached, first, for the newspaper, then a coffee mug or a shot glass. She still smiled – a good sign. I preferred to view her wisecracks as kidding and not the first telling tick of the time bomb secreted inside her.

"You like Italian, don't you?" she asked.

"Very much."

"A feast is in order. Don't you think? It's bound to be some saint's holy day today, some poor, tortured son of a bitch ripped to shreds by hyenas to prove his love for God. Maybe today is Saint Fritz's Day."

"There is no Saint Fritz."

"Well, there needs to be. I'm proclaiming today Saint Fritz's Day."

"There's a Feast of Saint Frederick. That's my feast day. July 18."

"How did you know that?"

"I don't know. School, I guess."

"You know, your grandfather's name, my father, his name was Frederick. *Federico.* Fred in Italian. I named this dog after him." Then: "Didn't I?" to Fred in baby talk. He wagged his tail and mooned dreamily at her with her same brown eyes. My brown eyes. Federico's brown eyes. "After you, too, Fritz. I have both of my little Freds here with me in the kitchen. No big Fred though. I didn't like big Fred very much." She held up the hammer. "This is big Fred's cobbler's hammer."

Each time she said *Fred*, she pounded the flank steak with the hammer and a fleck of cigarette ash fell on the meat – and Fred the dog lifted his head from the sports page.

She paused and commanded: "Sit, Fred." Fred scrambled to his feet and sat before her in rapt attention. She laid down the hammer and put the gun to his head. Perfectly still, he stared longingly at her, over the bore, awaiting assassination, the muzzle between his eyes.

"Pow," she said in a monotone, and he died at her feet. She glanced at me, put up the gun, smiled, and snapped her fingers with her hand no longer a pistol. Fred came back from the dead and wagged his tail.

I went upstairs to change out of my church clothes. My dad was asleep in my bed.

"Why is Dad in my bed?" I asked when I returned to the kitchen.

"He's pouting. That's his new thing. Every day, when you get up, he crawls in your bed. He's jealous of my new beau here. Isn't he?" Again, she used the sing-song baby voice. Fred shimmied and wagged.

"He's worried I'll leave him for this dog. But all men are dogs. Why leave one for another?" She dropped a hunk of raw meat to Fred that he swallowed whole. He had ignored me since I walked in the house.

She layered each tongue of steak with olive oil, garlic, parsley, salt, and pepper, scrolled them into bales, fastened them with string from Stagno's Bakery, and dropped them into the sauce.

"You want a meatball?" she asked.

"You made meatballs?"

"Jesus, Fritzy. Do I look like someone who wouldn't make meatballs on Saint Fritz's Day?"

She fished two meatballs out of the sauce. One she dropped on the floor for Fred, who instantly devoured it, then licked the sauce from the floor. The other she skewered with a fork and handed to me. I sat at the kitchen table and scouted for booze. Not a trace of it anywhere. My parents never hid their drinking. I watched the snow fall, the apron knot at my mother's hips, her frizzy hair pinned up, the innocent girlish nape of her bare neck, cigarette smoke crowning her, Fred now fast asleep, whimpering as his eyes rolled beneath his fastened lids. The kitchen had been painted yellow, who knows how long ago, way before we had rented the place. It was now like one big nicotine stain, the jaundiced plaster cracked in the cornices, the molding buckled.

I was rarely alone with my mother, and she was rarely this affable, if I can even permit myself to use this word to describe her – and she had had nothing to drink, as far as I could determine – so I decided to tell her about glimpsing my grandfather that morning in Cici's store lintel.

"Mom, today when I was on my way to Mass" – I realized I had no affectionate name attached to my mother's father – no *Grandpa*, or *Grandpap, Papa, Nonno* – "I thought I saw – I know I saw – your father, my grandfather, Big Fred, sitting on that slab at the entrance to Cici's."

She turned from stirring the sauce, elevated prophetically the wooden spoon, dripping red coins on the lily-patterned linoleum, and said, "Oh, my God," before sinking into the chair across the table from me. Stricken, she laid the still-dripping spoon on the table, lit another cigarette – one still burned on the counter – took a few drags, and snapped her fingers. Fred instantly awoke, lapped up the spilled coins, stepped to her, and rested his head in her lap. She felt about his face as one might a feverish, anxious child, dipped and kissed him, smoked a little more, dabbed out the cigarette in the ashtray, reached across the table for my hand, held it – surely the first time my hand had been in hers since I was a child – and finally whispered: "Tell me about it. Please, Fritzy."

In that moment, something had softened in my mother. I'd seen it before, something that surfaced when she was most herself, at her saddest, but frequently most dangerous in the bargain. I'd probably made a dreadful mistake broaching this, but there was nothing for it now but to go on.

I told her what had happened – though I left out the dying dog and the black children – that Federico smoldered in his finely tailored suit of embers and smoking fedora, his jaw a stubbled goblet of flint, the stench of immolation hovering him. That, for a moment, the sky had charred. That I had not been afraid. That he was there, then he wasn't there. That it had begun to snow – the same snow falling outside our kitchen window, and all through East Liberty.

I did not mention that when I walked into the

church, the congregation had risen, and Father Giusina, swallowed in alb and cope, the glad green liturgical vestments to commemorate the feast of a venerable saint, emerged jittering from the sacristy, followed by the crucifer and acolytes. Nor that the nave and transoms quaked when the gorgeous blond Irish organist, Miss Claire, with whom I was in love, but had finally despaired of marrying – brokenhearted because I knew I'd never have her or her like – treadled and pressed out the first tremulous chords of *Asperges Me*. Nor that, at that instant, Father Giusina and his retinue knelt, and he sprinkled the chancel with his silver scepter, then in Gregorian chant croaked out "Asperges me, Domine," and Miss Claire revved the organ to transports, and the choir, like a battalion of conspiring angels, took it up. Nor that I had nearly fainted, yet still I had smelled my smoldering grandfather, but it had to have been the frankincense seething from the thurible or simply the aftermath of my longing and loneliness. Mere days before, I had been publicly decimated in a gymnasium, in a strange borough just outside of Pittsburgh, filled with strangers who cheered when that other boy forced me down and I had been powerless to move – and it had never once occurred to me to pray. Nor did I confess to my mother my loneliness or that other boy, the champion, I was certain she coveted rather than me.

She removed her hand from mine only to light cigarette after cigarette. Each time she spun the Zippo flywheel with her thumb across the flint, the spark igniting the butane rushing up the wick, I smelled my grandfather. I said nothing of the time as a little boy at North Park when my grandfather had appeared and urged me across the creek. Nor did I mention walking into Cici's after Mass.

"That's so beautiful, Fritz," she said, when I finished. "I dream about my father all the time, or maybe they're not dreams. Maybe they're visions. I'm not sure of the difference. But, because of your grandfather, you're sitting in that chair across from me." She noticed that her last sentence confused me and said, "I'll explain, but I think I'm going to have a little drink first." It was two o'clock on the nose, the day already darkening. The troposphere emptied its hourglass of snow. The sauce bubbled in the pot. Fred had gone back to sleep, mewling fitfully as if snared in a bad dream. "Reach me that bottle of VO in the cabinet above the stove – and splash a tiny bit of water in a glass, please?"

I got up and glanced through the dining room toward the stairs. I wanted my father, still asleep in my little bed, to walk in the room. I sat again and placed in front of my mother the glass with an inch of water in it, and the bottle of Seagram's VO. She lit another cigarette, clouded brown the water with a long pour of tepid whiskey, took my hand again, and began.

On December 23, 1953, her incinerated father appeared to her in a dream in her bedroom on Omega Street, where she still lived with her mother, Ouma, my grandmother – just the two of them. My mother's three brothers had already left home. At the time, she worked as a receptionist for a Jewish optometrist named Sheldon Roth on Highland Avenue next to Foxx's, the bar outside of which she and my father had discovered Fred two weeks earlier, and where my father had then been tending bar.

In the dream, Federico had been surrounded by flames, like some maniacal icon. The room reeked of brimstone, yet it grew unbearably cold. There was a chorus of writhing souls from Purgatory and the requisite vision of the Blessed Virgin – tired, wan, weeping Mary. From Federico's pores chuffed smoke. The suspiration of fire pinned my mother to her bed. The room dwindled of oxygen. Federico removed his fedora, brimmed with fiery coals. He seemed about to speak, to finally divulge something to his only daughter. She had no recollection of a single sentence from his mouth while he had lived – merely the grinding, rusted gutturals of a mute. But the dead are sworn to solemn oaths of silence – the condition whereby they are permitted return to earth – the same oath Federico had seemingly taken in life.

He had been about to share with her a secret about what had happened that day on Station Street when his cobbler's shop burnt – to perhaps deliver finally the last syllables of inscrutable Napolitano dialect, cast in fire, at the moment of his immolation, cauterized in his sealed mouth for a decade and a half.

But Ouma had swept into the room, wearing Federico's clothes, her habit once he had died. Ouma, the beautiful gypsy – too dark even to be Sicilian or Calabrese, the blood her tint was blamed on, how her caramel complexion was explained away. The same blood that quickened my mother, the blood she denied. Ouma, the quadroon, of ancestry spurious as Fred the dog's, whom my mother hated and worshiped – of whom I had only dreamy, sweet memories – a woman in the livery of a dead man. Ouma, an agent of the afterlife, had merely raised the window to the frozen night and let the living world into the room, thus banishing my grandfather that December night in 1953 when he arrived burning at my mother's bedstead.

My mother had not been grateful for her mother's intercession. She had not wanted to be delivered but carried away by whatever her father had come to share. The snowy morning after Federico's visitation,

December 24, she confided every bit of her dream to my Irish father, there behind the bar at Foxx's, a rag to swab it with over his shoulder, gaping at her as if a deranged statue had just taken life before his eyes and spoken in a clairvoyant voice. The barflies in Foxx's never looked up from their shots and beers. Freaks and seers were a dime a dozen in East Liberty.

At that time, 1953 – maybe even now – my dad was connected to petty bookmakers and numbers runners, knocking down when he could for extra bread. A little side job. My mother knew this about him – the network of innocent crimes, harmless moonlighting, was well-publicized in East Liberty – so she asked him to play a number for her: 311 – Federico's birth date, March 11, and coincidentally, or providentially, the address of his shop, 311 Station Street. A cherished superstition among Italians in East Liberty was if you dreamt of the dead, then the instant you opened your eyes the next morning, you sought out a bookie and played the stiff's birth date. Formulaic, sure to hit. My dad handed Philly Decker, an apprentice racketeer at his usual station on the sidewalk outside the bar, a five-dollar bill and a slip of paper with 311 circled on it. And, of course, the number hit, as was foretold, straight-up, for $400 – a pile of dough in '53. Rita Schiaretta was over like a fat rat.

My mother paused in the tale, lit another Chesterfield, dumped two more fingers of VO in her glass, unknotted her piled hair so that it fell in scorched, teased tangles about her face and neck, and suddenly she took on the dire existential madness of Marlena Dietrich's Lola Lola in *The Blue Angel.* Then she coiled up theatrically from her chair and snagged a long Cozzini knife from the cabinet drawer.

My mother with a knife in her hand – how she

clenched it in her fist – was rather mythic, operatic. Like Clytemnestra or Charlotte Corday – at the very edge of irrevocable. A spectral light flared inside her; she became incandescent. She heard voices, and, often, if you were in the room with her when she had her hand on the hilt, you heard them, too. Who would she stab? My father? Me? Herself? In rages, she had left knives quivering in walls, in doors, in the cabinets and tables. The knife like a torch, a lightning rod, a final exclamation point, the raised blade of love and hate, Abraham pacing toward Isaac on the sacrificial tablet.

She said nothing, merely looked at me, cigarette dangling from her unlipsticked mouth, looked through me, really, acid *drip-drip-dripping* off the stalactites leeched to the ceiling of her memory, the stereoscope into her past flashing in her pupils.

Thank God, Fred began to howl – this mournful wolf-wail, as if he'd been invaded by the same vision as my mother – and she jolted back to herself. She dropped to the floor with howling, moaning Fred and cooed, "There now. Mama wouldn't hurt her good boy," caressed and hushed him until he slept, eyes darting behind his closed lids, flanks beating like bellows.

She rose, the knife still in her hands, and said, "I was just getting ready to slice the eggplant," winked at me, and returned to the counter. She took up the two blindingly purple-black eggplant, so like a woman's breasts, stripped them of their hides – her face reflected in their sheen, stripped that away as well – down to the white flesh, rounds the size of the host at the Minor Elevation. Then salted and tiered them in the colander, weighted them with a six-pound tailor's Sad iron – from Formicola, the Napoli village where Federico was whelped – to draw out the bitterness before she fried them, and placed a saucer beneath the colander to accept the crimson liquor.

She turned to me, winked again, mugging, and asked: "Where was I?"

With the $400, Travis and Rita determined to drive out of that Christmas Eve snowstorm in Shelly Roth's borrowed Caddy to New Jersey. My mother had never seen the ocean, and my father regaled her with stories of its splendor and – already in love with her – had more or less begged her until she gave in to his pleas to ride off to the Atlantic with him. My mother drove.

"Your father is some poet, Fritzy," she said – a little wistfully, a little admiringly. "A real operator. Your father had never driven a car, something I didn't mind so much then," she couldn't refrain from throwing in. There had been a fifth of Four Roses in the front seat with them. New Jersey became Florida and Florida ended up a West Virginia blizzard and a cheap room at the Elk Motel, on the Elk River, in the one-horse town of Darden.

Not the first misdirection nor U-turn in the thousand divagations that Travis and Rita would stumble through in the succeeding days and years together. What my mother did not say is that night in the Elk Motel, on a bed, literally made to vibrate, ostensibly for therapeutic purposes, by fitting two bits in a slot attached to it, I was conceived.

Those moments in the car and, later in Darden, West Virginia, an unlikely Appalachian holler quilted in snow, Christmas Eve, 1953, were the happiest your father and I would ever be in our long and convoluted bargain. Nor did my mother say this, her back to me as she performed the ritual of the eggplant, the sauce roiling like an oracle, infiltrating the house with its perfume, smoke from her Chesterfield leaking portentously above her nimbus of bleached hair, while

Fred, her baby, lay sound asleep at her feet.

She turned – smiling again, sauce splashed across the front of her apron – and asked, "Did you pray for your mother today at Mass?"

"I always pray for you."

"What did you pray for?

"For you?"

"What words did you use when you talked to God about me?"

This is when my mother was at her most dangerous – when she played the *Whatever You Say Will Be Precisely Wrong and I'll Crucify You for It* game.

"What did you say about me to God, Saint Fritz?"

"What was that all that racket about?" asked my father, suddenly in the kitchen, bare-chested, barefooted, in his pajama bottoms, holding the decimated remnants of the *Press*.

"What racket, Travis?" My mother, with that long knife in her hand, walked two paces to my father and kissed him sweetly on his mouth.

"All that caterwauling and howling."

"Poor Fred had a bad dream," said my mother.

"Hi, Dad."

"Good afternoon, Fritz." He rubbed his hand through my hair and smiled, dropped the newspaper on the table, grabbed what was left of my mother's drink and drained it in one swallow. "Smells rapturous in this house, Rita. What's gotten into you? Has someone died?" He kissed her, and they smiled at each other.

"I had the *voigla*, Travis. You know what that is, don't you?"

"I don't think I do, Rita."

"Desire. Craving. For Italian food. Today is Saint Fritz's Day, and we're going to celebrate."

"That's fine by me," said my dad, sinking into the

chair across from me and lighting one of my mother's cigarettes.

Fred lifted his head and looked at my father.

"Hello, Fred," said my dad. He reached down and patted Fred.

"Did you know, Travis, that there is no Saint Travis? But there is a Saint Rita."

"Of course, there's a Saint Rita, Rita. It's you."

"And you are full of shit, No-Saint Travis."

"Saints don't typically use that kind of language, Rita."

"Well," said my mother, "Saint Rita was a coarse Italian, if that explains anything, always pissed off at the vicious, idiot men in her life, so she found a lot of comfort in swearing. She's the patron saint of abused wives and heartbroken women. You can look that up."

"And profanity?" said my dad.

"Maybe. My mother forced me to dress like Saint Rita for Halloween. Here's what I looked like." My mother grabbed the soiled tea towel from the oven handle, draped it over her head and knotted it beneath her chin. She dipped into the red-hot sauce with her bare fingers and smeared twin gashes of it across her forehead. "For Saint Rita's stigmata," she said. "My mother used rouge."

"You must have won the prize every year, Saint Rita."

"Saint Rita was also a nun," said my mother. "I hate nuns. Who did you dress up like on Halloween, No-Saint Travis?"

"Al Capone."

"Hah," exclaimed my mother. "Fred," she said, and slapped her thigh. Fred marshaled to his feet and assumed his station before her, the pistol cocked at her side. "Any last words, Fred?"

Fred contemplated a rejoinder, something for his epitaph, but he could only emit that same grinding yawp my mother had once described as her father's voice.

"Fritz prayed for me in church today." She held the gun on Fred, as he looked worshipfully up at her.

"That's a good thing to do," said my father.

"But he won't tell me exactly what he said to God on my behalf."

"Prayer's a private matter, Rita," said my dad.

"I don't like people saying things behind my back. Spilling secrets."

"All I said was 'Bless Mom and Dad.'"

"That sounds like a reasonable prayer, Fritz," said my dad. "I appreciate the thought."

"You said more than that, I'd bet," said my mother. "Swear to God that that's all you said to God about me. Raise your hand and swear."

There was a time, when I was younger, when my dad would have told my mother to drop it, to let up. But I would be fifteen in September. I was in high school. He didn't want to interfere. And there was also the matter of my recent defeat in the tournament. It was not so much that my father wanted me to be a man. He didn't go in for that jingoistic shit. But he understood what it took to be a man – not swagger or even bravery – but a kind of constancy, conviction, even if that conviction was that you were not brave, that you didn't have what it takes. But you had to be true. My dad was letting me know that he had confidence that I could settle this just as well, if not better, than he could. He had plenty of experience with these ambushes – my mother's ploys, the games she masterminded. But he had just been jerked from sleep by a howling dog his wife had named after his dead father-in-law as well as his son, then rolled into the kitchen, and was confronted by my mother under one of her demonic spells, brandishing a knife, on tiptoe, kissing him. He was leaving this one up to me.

"Raise your hand and swear, Saint Fritz, on your feast day, that I created in your honor, that that's all you said."

I thought back to the Mass, but an hour earlier, and what I might have laid on God as I sat in the nave under the chandeliers, the sad, Byzantine stained glass twitching holographically, the mummified statues on their plinths, tapers wiggling flame, frankincense drugging me, Miss Claire stories above in the gothic choir loft sipping her chaste breath, closing her turquoise eyes, before engaging the three-ton organ in the heaving prelude to *Holy God.* On his mammoth golden altar cross, Jesus lifted his head from his chest and gazed apathetically through the rose window in the narthex gable at the snow falling on Larimer Avenue.

Above the commingled voices of the choir and congregation, Miss Claire's soprano spread its blue mantle over me. A blast of bloody light splashed the chancel walls. For an instant, I had been blinded by ecstasy and heartbreak, the ineffable pathetic beauty of sacrifice. I understood perfectly why martyrs gave in to the hallucinogenic temptation to throw themselves into pits of ravenous dogs, and I began to cry softly, happier perhaps than I had ever been. I glided from the pew and queued with the others toward the altar for the Eucharist and its sanctifying grace. What I had murmured to God: that I wanted my parents there with me, that I wanted to not be so lonesome without them in that moment, that I wanted to marry Miss Claire.

I raised my right hand, as directed by my mother, and told her that very thing: certainly not all of it – that would have been a little too much for them – but merely that I had missed having them there with me in church – as a family, if you will – and that I had indeed said to God, rather unoriginally, as one says, the meager prayer, "Bless Mom and Dad."

Rita pulled the trigger, and Fred collapsed.

Then my mother trained the gun on me and my father. Rita Sweeney, Saint Rita: in nightgown and apron, the impress of divine favor slashed between her eyes, her cigarette smoke inscribing the dying light, the sauce she had prepared from old blood secrets bubbling, with a gun in her hand pointed at her husband and only child. Breathtaking. But *Jesus Christ!* My father and I never loved her more – or saw so clearly the inevitable demolition.

My dad was cool as a cucumber, Travis Sweeney to the nines, on the surface, but braced for her next move. She was so perversely imaginative – a gift that additionally endeared her to my dad. "Go ahead and shoot, Rita," he said.

"I'm not going to shoot anybody," she said. "Just myself." Then she put the gun to her temple.

"Jesus God, Rita," said my dad.

My father and I sat there, utterly still.

Finally, my mother removed the gun from her head and set the knife on the table. "We need bread," she said gently. "I think I'll take the dog for a walk and pick up a loaf at Stagno's."

"I'll go, Mom," I said.

"No, no, I think a little walk is just what the doctor ordered."

"Honey," said, my dad, "why not let Fritz go? It's bitter out there and snowing."

"You're both being sweet to me. I understand what just happened. But I need to take the air, and Fred needs a walk. I'll fry the eggplant when I get back."

Fred, never summoned back to the world of the living, still lay where he fell, obediently dead, crossed over, for the past many minutes.

"Fred," my mother said, and snapped her fingers.

It was then I remembered how I knew Fred. I had seen him on Omega Street, in DiDomenis' back yard. Mrs. DiDomeni's mysterious husband was black or Spanish. He drove a tractor-trailer rig and was rarely at home. In early December, he had arrived with a doe he had pierced through its heart with an arrow and hung her upside down, gutted, in the DiDomenis' yard from a chain dangling from an oak. The arrow still protruded, its bright red fletching an inch from her pretty coat.

Fred was among the dogs mobbed beneath the carcass the night Mrs. DiDomeni's husband strung it up. Initially, the dogs simply sat, perfectly still, and longingly stared at the doe's spellbinding, glassy brown eyes, open, above them. Then they sang and leapt up and ripped at her. I knew some of them: gypsies, grifters, lonely hearts, freaks, hoods, *gavones*. Dogs in East Liberty came and went, strangers slipping in, living in alleys and sewers, under the bridges, down the Hollow, on Larimer Avenue along the backyards of row houses. Sometimes they were taken in. But most of those dogs drifted off, after something they imagined was better, and we never saw them again. Some ended up dead – like the dog in front of the rectory – or executed by the dog catcher, or poisoned by those who hated them for simply being alive.

Fred had caught my eye that day because he seemed so hesitant – so good-looking (and he knew it) – his pretty white face and brown ears, brilliant eyes. But Fred was wary of the other dogs. He knew he was a dog. He knew what that meant. He wanted their respect, but he was not like them. They tore so viciously at the doe –

she never looked away – but Fred, while he jumped and cried out, did not bite her. Mrs. DiDomeni's husband charged out of the house with a baseball bat, and the dogs, including Fred, scattered.

That day I had seen Fred among the other dogs, I sensed his broken heart, that he was way too sensitive. Cap pistols or the old Italian ladies haggling with the huckster over artichokes scared him. One day, after Fred had come to live with us, my mother screamed: the lightbulb in the refrigerator had blown. That my mother screamed because of the lightbulb did not strike my father and me as odd. My mother habitually screamed in displeasure. But Fred went to pieces – hit the floor, prone, cowering. like a soldier in the shit too long.

"Fred," my mother said, and snapped her fingers again.

Fred didn't move. He didn't breathe.

"Fred." She said it louder. Then much louder: "Fred, Fred, Fred!"

Fred didn't move.

Then my dad, not shouting, "Fred," but close to it – on his feet and down with Fred, checking to see if he was alive, if he was breathing.

"I killed him," my mother said – her voice raw wire, awful to hear. "I finally got what I wanted. Oh, Jesus Christ! I'm being punished."

You can't murder someone by pointing your finger at him and saying *Pow*, but my mother had miraculously done it – like some crazy tale from the Old Testament. My father removed his hand from Fred's side. He rose and turned to her, and said "Sweetheart," as she receded, as if in the grip of a tractor beam, growing smaller, younger, dimmer, the pilot guttering, a haunting omniscient smile on her face. She was departing. How many times had she said she could no longer take it – and now she could no longer take it. My father and I were losing her. Neither of us uttered a syllable. This was the end of my mother, so much more peaceful than I had ever imagined.

Fred, the dog, had been playing possum, or maybe the spell my mother had put him under had worn off. He bounded up, yawned and stretched, glanced at my dad and me, then found my mother and drew her back to us with his eyes until she was on the floor with him, holding him to her as if he were someone she had known and lost a very long time ago, and Fred, astonished, madly in love with her.

My dad and I got down there with her, hugged and petted Fred, and welcomed him back, our good boy. There were elements of living in our house that hadn't been easy for him, either. He was as undone by my mother as we were.

"You still have the power of life and death, Rita," my dad said, put his arm around her, and kissed her hair.

"I have to go, Travis," she said.

"You don't have to go anywhere, Rita."

"I'm taking Fred for a walk and buying a loaf of bread for supper."

"Fritz'll go. I'll go," said my dad. "We don't need bread. It's bitter out there. Sit down and have a drink, Honey. I'll finish cooking."

"Please stay here, Mom."

For a moment, she relented. The spirit coursed visibly through her, illuminating her, softening her. She smiled; the kitchen pulsed with light. She had decided we really did love her. She was going to stay home.

Then she said, "I'll do as I please," fastened Fred to his leash, tugged on boots, threw a coat over her nightgown and apron, and they rumbled through the back door – the stigmata slashed across her brow, the tea towel wimple bundled about her head.

"Jesus Christ," my dad said a few moments later – we had been gaping at one another across the table since my mother left the house with Fred – "she doesn't have gloves."

Stagno's Bakery was at best, round-trip, about a quarter mile from our house: down Saint Marie, then a very long block down Collins, and a left at Hoeveler. Stagno's perched just at the edge of the Hoeveler Street Bridge – the bridge Mickey D'Andrea had fallen from and paralyzed himself. But my mother, for whatever reason that late afternoon, night falling, did not take the direct route. Beyond our tiny yard was a hundred-foot drop into crabapple thickets; weeds; an appliance graveyard; all manner of unpredictable, often thrilling trash; tree houses crowded with bums and gypsies; the carcass of every spent East Liberty Christmas tree in the past century; finally, a creek, that day frozen solid – and then *Basa la Vallone,* christened by the first Italians who showed up in East Liberty. It means literally in English: "it bases valley." Everyone simply called it The Hollow.

It was indeed a hollow, through which Negley Run Boulevard drilled, the undeclared demilitarized zone that separated the Harriet Tubman Projects from the Italian stronghold that began on the cliffs of Collins Avenue. The Italians and Blacks had clashed over the years, two diasporic sets of refugees, every bit as reviled as Fred and his ilk. Nevertheless, they had settled on hating each other, and their antipathy took literal fire during the riots in 1968 that followed the murder of Martin Luther King. During the riots and the ensuing curfew, my dad, at my mother's insistence, had even borrowed a gun; and, for all I knew, it was still in the house. My dad was at heart a pacifist, someone who characteristically avoided trouble of any sort, even if he had married a live grenade.

It was a quiet, peaceful day – my mother did not see another human – perhaps in deference to the Sabbath, but more likely because of the snow and insane cold. She minced down the slick slope, Fred on his leash, nosing about, yanking her. Several inches of dirty slush, refrozen again and again, lay across the earth. The scrub trees were laced in snow. She reached for them with her free hand and slalomed among them, a crisscross, fitful gait to keep her balance. Blackbirds called.

She cried a bit. Maybe she prayed, though I had never seen her publicly pray – we didn't even say grace at the lone meal we had together during the week – though she was a believer. A winter finch fluttered across the crusted snow. Fred broke for it, dragging my mother. She skated down the iced slope, then upended and came down hard on her back, the wind knocked out of her, perhaps knocked unconscious, then rolled fifty feet until she snagged in a dead burdock and lay there, not far from the lip of Negley Run. Snow fell relentlessly, straight as a plumb line, down upon her face, her eyes wide open to receive it.

When my mother came around and gathered herself, Fred was gone, and she was banged up, scratched and bruised, but not bleeding. Her icy hands had gnarled into claws. She stuffed them in her coat pockets and struggled to her feet.

"Fred," she called. "Fred, Fred, Fred. Please, Fred." Then she collapsed in the snow and cried. At that point in my life, six months shy of my fifteenth birthday, I had never seen her cry. But inside her was a river driven by incessant weeping – and that day she cried for Fred, her good boy, her only boy, and pleaded with him to come back to her. But, of course, there was so much more that she wept over, as there always is.

All that returned to her as she lay there was the sound of her voice – a pretty voice, a soft voice, for such a singularly hard woman. But, in truth, Rita Schiaretta Sweeney was not hard at all but rather the victim of one sucker punch too many. She relied on scorn to surmount hardship. She spat in the eye of hardship. *Give me more,* she demanded of it habitually – though she could not bear any more – and hardship complied, stood her another round, and she ingested it like the gall proffered Jesus on a spearhead, as he writhed on the cross. Bitterness sustained her – all the times she'd been wronged and misunderstood. But she did not want to be that way. My father claimed that we are all two people – which I believe – and often those two people, the good and the bad, live simultaneously joined like Siamese twins, though strangers, not even on speaking terms.

Still, she cried, "Fred, Fred," things clouding together – too many secrets, too much silence, snow falling in sheer curtains – and she remembered the red car coat she had worn that late December day in 1953 when she waltzed into Foxx's and asked Black Irish Travis Sweeney to play a number for her: indescribably soft Italian lamb's wool that fell at the knee, single-needle topstitching and black horn buttons. With her first paycheck from Shelly Roth, she put it on layaway at Lerner's for three dollars and paid eight months on it until she took it home.

How handsome Travis had been, behind the bar with a rag over the shoulder of his blinding white shirt, his then full head of curly black hair and pretty blue eyes. He was so much more than those rummies on their stools, taller and stronger, smarter by half and then some. He saw through everything, including her, and never tried to hustle her. No one had ever loved her like Travis. Maybe no one else had ever loved her before him. And Travis had fallen for her – like the snow fell. She had been unkind to Travis over the years, abusive even, her *gutless wonder*, railed that he was spineless. *Pigshit Irish*. Even accused him of being queer. Had she ever told Travis Sweeney she loved him? Surely. But piss on that. Regret: *rimpianto*. For the frail, the weak. "Fred," she screamed. "Baby. Fred." What had happened to that coat?

She crossed under the Hoeveler Street Bridge, limped left at Hamilton Avenue, lingered, with numb fingers managed to light a cigarette, and sat on the top step of Bagnio Vicas's barber shop stoop, wedged in the nexus of Hoeveler, Hamilton Avenue, and Omega Street, under the striped whirling red, white, and blue barber pole – a symbol dating back to the medieval barber's shingle, when barbers not only cut your hair, but let your blood. Thus, the red, and the white for bandages, and the blue for who knows what. Maybe the raw case of blues she was born with, maybe Travis's blue eyes. No, she knew what it was: the bitter, blue, cold world. Rita shuddered in its might and took a drag. Bagnio Vica: what a *gavone* operator. She would have never fallen for his line of shit, so mad about himself – pretty boy vamp. Pimp. He tried to put the make on bobbysoxers on their way to Divine Providence Academy next to a convent. Even the nuns, God forbid, weren't safe around him. She tried to smile and realized there was blood in her mouth, scouted with her tongue to account for her teeth. "Fred," she called. "Fred, Fred, Fred."

She had to get the bread. But she was so roughed up, beaten, the way it hurts when someone who knows how works you over. Through the snow, Stagno's light was visible from where she sat – just past the listing, shuttered Spignos Club, a flatiron of Carrara marble and Tuscan tile, about to plunge into the Hollow, on the other side of Hoeveler Street, at the far end of the bridge that crazy artist kid, Mickey D'Andrea, had plummeted from. That had to have been ten years ago. Everyone explained away his crash into the boulevard as a daredevil stunt gone bad, an accident, but bridges and kids falling from them had become a trope in East Liberty. Then she worried about me, her kid, at the age where boys' bodies catch up with their desires, but their impulses remain mired in the infantile – one hand in their pants, the other on a blow torch.

Maybe she had been too hard on me, she thought – about the wrestling – but goddammit, I had to be a man, not like my dad. She had come to one of my matches, despite my forbidding her to ever show up, in a leopard dress, hair teased into a crazy orange tangle, and half wig or something crawling down her back, made up like Salome, an unlit Chesterfield between her lips. She screamed for me to massacre my opponent. "Kill him," over and over – all eyes on her rather than the mat. Standing in the bleachers screeching for annihilation – like it was all on me to murder whatever she felt the world had cheated her of.

I was expected to bristle and break jaws, wear leather, take sharp turns on two wheels in a muscle car, someday beat the shit out of her brothers – whom she barely spoke to – especially Patrick, seven years older than her, who had come back from the war a hero and built a million-dollar brick outfit out of a second-hand pickup truck and now lived in Rowena Township and lorded it over everyone. She switched on the stereoscope in her head and replayed that son of a bitch Patrick undress her friend Haggy in Booze Alley, right in front of her, while on leave, days before he shipped out for Burma to fight with Merrill's Marauders – two years after Federico's Requiem. She had the *voigla* for revenge. *Rivincita.* Vendetta.

Patrick was Ouma's favorite. She had kept vigil on the porch daily for the mailman and Patrick's long war letters that she read to Rita, then wrote back to him with a Turkish fountain pen, the envelopes fastened with sealing wax smudged from the votives sputtering in every room on the altars she had mounted, homage to the Virgin, who visited Ouma regularly – Rita had seen her – to ensure Patrick's safe return. When the electricity was turned off because the Schiarettas could not pay the light bill, Ouma, with that same pen, wrote an entreaty to Eleanor Roosevelt, sealed it with consecrated wax, included a holy card of Our Lady of Perpetual Help, and received in return almost immediately a letter from the First Lady, two days after power was restored, that she framed and tacked above her bed next to the crucifix.

Then had come the news that Patrick was missing in action, and Rita was insane with grief – though she had total amnesia about her father's death, didn't even remember the funeral. But Patrick – who also knew the real story of the fire that had cooked Federico – had turned up, thank God, in a military hospital in British India, recovering after being gravely ill with malaria and amoebic dysentery. He been decorated for bravery at the Siege of Myitkyina.

My mother reveled in the thought of my going to war, a rainbow of medals ranked across my uniform when I triumphantly returned to Saint Marie Street a hero. But then, with a wave of panic, she wiped away that thought, took it all back *(No war, fuck bravery)* – even though she knew, maybe more than anything, that nothing can ever be taken back. Word was trickling in about East Liberty kids dead in Vietnam, about an army-green Ford Custom Sedan at the curb with the flag and the Department of Defense stationary they sent home instead of your son – Shotty Montesanto's son, Rocco, blown to bits at Hue.

She screamed for Fred and lit another smoke, her fingers so lifeless she brought the pack to her mouth and lipped out a cigarette. From Saints Peter and Paul's ten-story belfry 4:30 tolled. She made up her mind she'd apologize to my father and me when she got home, but that would never happen. An apology from my mother, especially, would have broken my already broken heart. What was it about me and my father that cherished that ponderous chip on her shoulder?

She had to bring home the bread, a loaf of Sicilian because she knew that was my favorite, even though it cost a little more. The bakery closed at five, and she had to fry the eggplant because it was Saint Fritz's Day. She contemplated the futility of it all. She thought of taking the bridge, simply diving off, but the Hoeveler Street Bridge didn't pack the altitude guaranteed to hurl you into the next life. It was just a bad luck bridge – a short fall to cripple or vegetate you, like what had happened to Mickey D'Andrea. She'd end up another East Liberty side-show in a wheelchair. A cautionary tale. A joke. Travis could wheel her out to the stoop every morning, a ratty afghan across her lap, to traumatize the kids on their walks to school. The way to go was the high bridges, Larimer and Meadow. Finish the job. Closed casket.

Francene Renzo's husband, another artist, a painter, an angel hoodlum, one of the good ones, stationed in Italy during the war, had first done it. The impresario of suicide, the East Liberty pioneer. He was attempting to fly. He had left that in the note to Francene, not long after their kid Bobby – four or five years older than I – was born. Bobby was in Vietnam. Francene's brother, Giovanni, had been killed fighting in North Africa. News of Giovanni had come just days after they'd fielded word that Patrick was safe. Francene's mother's hair had fallen out when the green government car glided to the curb and killed the engine.

Perhaps it was that whirling helix of red, white, and blue she sat beneath on Vica's icy stoop, or the knock on the head, or her inability to distinguish the past from the present – the ruthlessness of the weather, of fate – like prelude to a dream. She smelled her father before she saw him – the scent of smoke that can never be scrubbed away, perfumed, or painted over. He was suddenly there, as *spettri* are wont to appear, impervious to the cold, perhaps on his way home from the club yard and bocce, his Sunday ritual. He walked slowly, deliberately, his hands behind his back, a little drunk. Tendrils of smoke wafted from him, flame spouting in the seams and folds of his gray trousers, gray cardigan, gray fedora. Gray skin. Gray whiskey stubble. He smiled or grimaced – his teeth were gray – stopped in front of his daughter, and doffed his cauldron hat in the courtly manner of Old World men. His gray hair sparked. My mother rose and was instantly warmed.

"Papa," she whispered and began to cry.

He said nothing, returned his hat to his head, knotted his hands behind his back, and paced the incline up Omega Street. She flicked the spent butt into the street, slammed her useless hands in her pockets, and slogged behind him – past the Miglios, Perinos, DeNinnos, Marcheses, DiDomenis, Hilliards, Pagnottas, Marchesanos, Merlinos, Luccettis, Zottolas, the feral scrap lots, and Goodwin's garages.

It was full dark, streetlamps ablaze, snow visible in

their haloes, rushing, hushed – the street abandoned. My grandfather stopped in front of his home, 317½ Omega Street, a tiny two-story stone house with a magnificent sycamore, still dangling a few renegade racemes from its spring flowering; its bark in stripped scrolls beneath the snow; somewhere on its white breast, *Rita*, carved with a pen knife just weeks before Federico's shop had caught fire – though she had long forgotten digging into the tree with what she'd hoped then, in a moment of girlish joy that spring of 1942, would remain a record that she had once walked the earth and had had a name, something indelible to return to.

A light shone in the lone upstairs window, her mother's bedroom. Federico turned to stare at the light.

"Papa," invoked my mother, but by then he had departed through the curtain of snow, and she heard an old Italian song, *"Ehi Cumpari,"* my mother swore Federico had sung to her when she was a *bambina*.

My father and I sat silently at the kitchen table. He had pieced together the tatters of the Sunday paper and read it, occasionally clipping coupons or a recipe. He drank coffee laced with apricot brandy and smoked cigarettes. The kitchen had grown dark with the dwindling day. We were no longer able to make out, through the window, the falling snow. I was trying to write a paper for English class that Brother Benedict had assigned on the "The Road Not Taken," by Robert Frost.

I was certain that I understood the poem, its message, its moral, the metaphor of the road, all that bullshit, but I was fed up, too. The poem struck me as a little too simplistic, at least for an East Liberty kid, conceived by Travis and Rita Sweeney on a vibrating motel bed next to a frozen river in the godforsaken West Virginia mountains, a kid who started out a certified bastard. I wanted to be straight-up in the paper, unload it all on Brother Benedict, give him a heart-to-heart thumbnail of the various crossroads I had paused at and stumbled through, a good few of them in my head and heart, another terrifying handful in my soul – I would soon divest myself of the sacramental life, all that really mattered to me about Catholicism – and then there were all those very real crossroads. Like: You walk out my front door and step off the stoop and you're literally at the crossroads of Saint Marie and Meadow Street, not exactly "two roads [diverging] in a yellow wood," but more like a big, stinking concrete package of danger, where you take your not at all metaphorical, but very real, flesh-and-blood life into your hands, depending on which way you turn, especially if you're some white half-Irish, half-Italian kid – with a secret chalice of black genes lurking in him, too – who can't fight and can't play ball and in truth doesn't know shit from Shinola, yet has hair sprouting all over his body and, most of the time, is confused and ashamed and afraid to ask questions, his own kitchen a cocked and loaded gun.

What do you do? This way or that? It depends who you'd prefer to get your ass kicked by: the pissed-off blacks or the pissed-off Italians? You go left at Saint Marie, and you deal with the wasted hoods with their switchblades, homemade zip guns, and tattoos, and poor-boys of cheap, nasty, sweet red wine – and dope. Not just reefer and keef, hashish and glue, but heroin. Tying off and tapping a vein. Junk. Smack. Half of them artists, the other half gangsters, and plenty that are both. On mellow days, in their black leather jackets and little pimp Trilbys made famous by Frank Sinatra, they might just nod, even smile, offer you a hit, try and bum a cigarette, even kid around. But, if the jonesing, tortured Muse had its talons in them, they would shake you down for change or sucker punch you. Kick you when you're down. They might pull a switchblade.

If you make a right and cross the Meadow Street Bridge – a big, high bridge, the one Bobby Renzo's dad threw himself off one night in his pajamas – you're headed for dead-on-arrival. The blacks, burnished in fear and anger, at the other end of that bridge, if you make it to the other end, still lived in the charred ramparts of the '68 riots – still beside themselves with prophetic grief at the death of King, in their devotion to self-immolation, fanatically fatigued with the vicious white race, and now backed into those last, blasted blocks of East Liberty. And fucked up, just like their Italian doppelgängers on the white side of the bridge – on whatever death or amnesia they can slide into their bodies.

If you really wanted Frost's "yellow wood," there was yet another road that joined Meadow and Saint Marie: Stanton Avenue, off which rose way-the-hell up, at a perfect forty-five degrees, Heberton Street and then Highland Park – where you take your chances with the rich, like crashing Heaven without papers: the doctors and lawyers who belonged to country clubs and the Pittsburgh Athletic Association, where they signed for everything; and their blond kids who went to the Ellis School and Winchester Thurston and Kiski Prep and Shadyside Academy, and went to summer golf and tennis camps; whose blond moms had cultivated tans and wore madras wraparound skirts and drove station wagons with wood siding and had black maids and gardeners, blenders and vermouth on their counters, and took long vacations next to the Atlantic Ocean.

My mother hated the well-to-do most of all. She saw them as her oppressors, their heels on her throat, the haughty unreachable precipice from which they looked down upon her and her kind. They wouldn't say shit if they had a mouthful. Those wasted beat hoods, black and white: she didn't trust them, but they had suffered. They ate their weight in shit every day they opened their eyes. My mother, Rita Sweeney – out there somewhere in a blizzard searching for a foundling dog she'd named after her dead father – gloried in suffering.

Maybe, in my paper, I'd lay all this on Brother Benedict, record in writing just the way it grabbed me. But really, I was that guy at the crossroads, right? Isn't that why Frost's poem was shoved down your throat at school? The guy in the poem pauses and ponders, then chooses presumably the correct path, "the one less travelled by," the one that ends up "[making] all the difference." So, if you have the good sense to choose the proper road, and if you have the time and money to stop and figure it all out, it will make "all the difference." But Frost never explains what "all the difference" is. Is "difference" good or bad? The poem is "The Road Not Taken" – not the "The Road Taken." The guy is "telling this with a sigh." He knows he fucked up. He knows he should have taken the other road, but he won't admit it. He is like my mother, like my father, too, like all of us. He has a head like a brick, and he would swear by his bad decisions, on his mother's eyes, till his dying day.

When my dad asked me what I was writing about and I told him, he recited flawlessly the entire poem, looking at me the whole time, with a slick little smile on his face.

"Dad," I asked, "how the heck did you do that?"

"I don't know," he said and winked. He confided that he could recite perfectly "Gunga Din," "The Charge of the Light Brigade," "The Song of Hiawatha," and Edgar Allan Poe's "Annabelle Lee," a poem Brother

Benedict had read to us, in which I had heard regret and longing – so beautiful.

"How do you like Frost's poem?" he asked.

I recapitulated in a roundabout way my basic take on it – without all the personal existential flourishes. By then, I had decided I could write a poem as good as Frost's. I was tired of his poem. I was tired of parables.

My dad listened and nodded. "That's a pretty sound assessment, Fritz. Life's a crapshoot. This way or that way. Who knows? We're at the mercy of random, but we like to pretend we have control. Most of the choices we make are irrational. We're all just trying to bear up and get down the road. A lot of promise and a lot of heartache on the way, but there's no use just sitting around, either. People take wrong turns all the time. You never realize your destination until you land at it, and you're about nuts when you arrive. Like Frost says, and this is my favorite line, 'way leads onto way.' We have absolutely no control. I'm not someone who feels comfortable giving advice, but what you want to steer clear of, like the plague, Fritz, is regret and, worse, bitterness. It's poison, and it poisons everyone around you. But you worry too much. Take a crack at life and see what happens."

I realized at that moment that I knew so little about my father's past. His mother and father were dead. I had never met them. He had no brothers or sisters. Unless he did. Unless his parents were still alive. I never knew what to believe, what was true. But here's what I knew about how "way leads onto way": In the next many months, a man would set foot on the moon; Woodstock staged; the Beatles, at Abbey Road, for the last time together; the revelation of the My Lai Massacre; the murders of Sharon Tate and the LaBiancas by the Manson Family. Ho Chi Minh and Jack Kerouac would die. Under the influence of ennui so profound, I would clandestinely leave the church. I could have asked my father anything, and he'd tell me the truth: about his mother and father; about the fire at Fred the Shoemaker's, how it started, what really happened – he knew the real story, or maybe he just thought he knew – but I let that opportunity pass like the ghost of my grandfather.

My mother, at that very moment, a few blocks from where we sat, mounted the three steps to the concrete and wrought iron porch of her childhood home on Omega Street. She was about to turn the brass knob of its front door. She had to see her mother. The light that had been on in the room above extinguished. Five o'clock knelled from the church bell towers across East Liberty.

Suddenly out of Booze Alley trotted a procession of dogs, all of whom I'd seen that day beneath the doe in DiDomenis' back yard: the Hunters' spaniel who'd bitten me over the eye the one time I remember visiting my grandmother with my mother, and I had to get a tetanus shot, and my mother went after Cleopatra Hunter with a knife she pulled out of her purse; Delilah, Wild Guglielmo's lascivious black German Shepherd, always chained, a skilled predator, though she dragged her broken chain like Jacob Marley; Nino, the Luccettis' dog, a creamed coffee-colored, horse-like mastiff from one of the provinces, that barked in dialect and unprovoked dragged small children by their ankles through the streets – though now lame, senescent, and trailed the others like a *straccione;* a contemplative, small, nearly all-black dog named Canto, a tiny white tab of fur stamped at his throat so he resembled a Jesuit; Figaro, a petite, unkempt poodle who liked to fight, whose pained bark sounded like a concertina; the red shepherd, King, driven mad by the noon air raid siren, who belonged to the regal French widow, Suzanne Marisse; the aged dogs from the old country, who walked slowly, dignified; the lost dogs; dogs that belonged to no one, nobody's children; the ghosts of dogs. Many of them were crazy, and everyone knew it. No different than with the crazy people.

Fred was among them: furtive, coy, suddenly a yearning teenage hoodlum – intoxicated with the lore of the avenue. But still a decent boy, a good boy, who had glimpsed for a fortnight, at our house on Saint Marie, what a real home – fraught with love and recrimination, raised voices, hideous secrets – might look like. But yet a home, nonetheless: a place to come to. There was still plenty of hope for him, but the portal was closing. The snow fell in torn shrouds. It was pitch dark and frigid.

Overjoyed to see Fred, my mother walked away from her mother's door and approached the pack of dogs, a number of whom were dangerous, but would not cross Rita Sweeney. She was afraid of nothing, and they knew it. They parted in her wake.

"Fred," she implored and attempted to kneel before him, but her feet and legs were numb. She fell into the snow at his feet and reached up to grasp his leash, sheathed in ice. But her frozen hands would not close over it. Fred sized up my mother, as if he didn't know her. The other dogs looked on. "Fred," she begged. "Please, Fred."

Fred loved my mother desperately, and perhaps he had been attempting, in his sheepish way, to tell us something, to literally speak, divulge the story of my grandfather and how his shop caught fire – unless, of course, my mother knew perfectly what had happened in 1942 on Station Street. That abiding secret was at the core of her misery, as well as the fact that she had nothing to do with her own mother, my grandmother. Rita, the only girl, had worked for her father: three bucks for all of Saturday – her brothers had never punched in for Federico – and she had been made to turn over every dime of it to her mother. Was she there when the fire started? Did she start the fire?

"Fred," she said one last time.

He showed his teeth and nipped at her; though, in the throes of frostbite, she wouldn't have felt it, just the snub, the kiss-off: *You're dead to me.* And, really, that was all she needed to make peace with Fred – a ritual parting, a requisite thimble of violent farewell.

But that's not what Fred had intended. He wanted to stay with my mother forever. He had never loved anything quite like her. But, out of instinct, he had learned one often trots away from what one loves most, from one's true love. He didn't understand it – he was a nearly fourteen-year-old boy – but he knew it was true. He had no choice but to obey the code. He would never have bitten my mother. He would have never hurt her. But he was so cold and scared and hungry in the dark on Omega Street in the bitter final days of that tragic steel town winter that had begun in 1968. *Fuck it,* he said to himself.

He gazed at my mother plaintively for a long time, then took off, stopped, looked back at her, turned and ran a few more paces – the snow was up to his nose as he plowed through it with difficulty – went on, stopped, looked back, again and again, until he halted at the mouth of Booze Alley – like the ghost of an old tortured Italian man, who had left behind his language and country a half century earlier – and fixed Rita Sweeney in *memento mori.* Then he churned off toward the church.

My mother – lying on the sidewalk in a foot

of snow, beneath her mother's blackened bedroom window, and the mythic sycamore that bore her girlhood's signet – said aloud: "Go ahead and leave. I never loved you. I don't need you." Fred was two-faced, ungrateful. She should have dumped him at the Animal Rescue League.

The door to 317½ Omega Street opened. My grandmother, Ouma, walked to her daughter Rita and knelt.

My father and I were still in the kitchen, throwing two-handed blackjack, gambling Diamond wooden kitchen matches used to light the pilot on our rickety gas stove. He had turned off and put a lid on the sauce, and tidied up the kitchen, placed the colander with the eggplant in the refrigerator.

"I'm going after your mother," he announced.

"I'll come with you, Dad."

"Stay here, Fritzy, and finish your homework. I'll be back in a flash." He bundled up and walked out the kitchen door.

I went back to writing the Frost paper, but then got scared. I was no stranger to being alone – I spent nearly every hour, except for school, by myself – but I had a very distinct sense of having been abandoned, finally abandoned, as if I had all along expected it. Inevitable. I hammered at the poem, but all those roads – the choices, the dead-ends, alleys, and one-way streets, the danger, the twisting plat of East Liberty, the tangle of routes that inexplicably knit and sundered everything at once, was simply beyond my ken.

My dad, on his mission to rescue my mother, had made it to the corner of Collins and Hoeveler.

My mother, now on her feet, scaled with the help of Ouma the porch steps of 317½ and entered the little house she had been born to, into the living room: the chartreuse chair my mother had read in as a child; the china toreador figurines from Pamplona, and tiny bells from all over the world that spread the mantle on doilies; hand-painted lamps with capering naked cherubim in porcelain relief; Persian throw rugs; faded, purple, fleur-de-lis wallpaper.

My mother allowed Ouma to help her out of her sodden clothes and into a silk challis, robe, and alpaca socks, sponge her scratched face with warm water, kiss her cheeks, lay her on the French divan, cover her with a Moroccan batik quilt, then put on the kettle. Rita had not been in this house for thirteen years. "Mama," she whispered.

Fred thrashed through the snow on frozen feet, looking back, looking back. Ice had clotted between his toes. He prized it out with his teeth. Like an umbilical cord, his leash trailed heavily, white and blood-red in the snow. He passed Cici's store. Federico, in his formal suit of smoke, wept beneath its shingle. Fred paused at the door and looked inside. Cici hoisted a withered, creased palm in farewell. The death of his *compadre*, Federico – the infamia of his fiery death – had silenced him.

At Saints Peter and Paul, a silent, twin-steepled monolith of snow, Fred bowed his head – *Mea Culpa, Mea Culpa, Mea Maxima Culpa* – and began the long trek down Larimer Avenue: the Italian *grocerias* and restaurants – Labriola's, Pompa's, Gigante's, Paradise's, Costa's, Geneviève's; beyond the club yard and Larimer school, abandoned, boarded houses, spackled in revolutionary graffiti; then Chester's gas station, his vicious twin Dobermans, the shackles they strained at, their murderous snarls as Fred slogged by them; and, finally, Henry Grasso's Sausage Shop at the very edge of the assassin Larimer Bridge, its maze of ramparts and parapets, illusory in the squall.

My father made the left on Hoeveler. He wore black buckle arctic boots to his knees and a massive black topcoat, black gloves, white scarf, and a charcoal brim-down fedora. It was well past five, no one else on the streets. The bakery was closed, but the light was still on, Mrs. Tommarello behind the counter, her black hair in a bun. Her glasses glittered. Her teeth glittered. She smiled when she spied my father in the snow, peering through the big front window, unlocked the door, and kissed him. She conversed with him in Italian, a language he was not completely ignorant of. It landed upon his ear like Pentecostal opera. Like machine gun fire. He flashed his most honorable smile. It was paramount he show respect. Mrs. Tommarello had unlocked the door of the bakery so that he might have bread in a blizzard. She reckoned the cross he bore in Rita Schiaretta. They kissed again as he departed.

Ouma kissed her daughter's frozen hands and wrapped them in uncarded wool. She spooned bouillabaisse from a gold and scarlet saucer into her daughter's chapped mouth. Rita raised her head from the pillow, looked into her mother's eyes, and parted her lips.

With the bread from Mrs. Tommarello, and a fresh rum cake, my father crossed the Hoeveler Street Bridge. He did not contemplate the abyss into which Mickey D'Andrea had vanished. At the nexus of Hoeveler, Hamilton, and Omega, at Bagnio Vica's barber shop, he paused and lit a cigarette. He took exactly three drags, threw down the cigarette – it glowed an instant red and was gone – then he trudged up Omega Street.

He nearly fell over my mother, lying beneath the sycamore that bore her faded name. 317½ Omega Street was vacant. Ouma no longer lived there. She had been dead three months. He crouched next to his wife, lifted her head from the snow, brushed snow from her face, and kissed her forehead. He removed his gloves and fit her fingers into them. Around her neck, he wound his scarf. Upon her head, he placed his hat. She awoke and put her arms around his neck. He cradled her in his arms, astonished she was so light, and stood, still clutching the cake and bread. My father held on to everything.

Exhausted and cold, Fred walked slowly. He turned left off Lemington and climbed Lincoln Avenue. The ascent was perilous, the icy wind in his face, the few cars that plowed by heavily chained. He hunkered like a wolf and dug his way up the cobblestones – past Joe Westray's Ebony Lounge, the Church of Corpus Christi, Saint Walburga's, and finally Saint Joseph's Military School – statues, stone, and stained-glass in the pitch, inside a brigade of nuns lording over hoodlum cadets – until Lincoln terminated and the streetcars finally died; and there, shrouded in the snowy gauze of amnesia, sprawled Mount Carmel Cemetery.

Fred hesitated at its enormous, black iron gates. The snow, beautiful on his coat, was so deep his brown tail brushed it as he crossed the sheeted graves and draped tombstones, chiseled with the names of the misremembered dead.

A monstrous ebony crucifix presided at the top of the hill, fastened to it an alabaster Christ, evanesced in the blizzard. Fred made for the cross and, at its foot, shivered, no longer visible.

My father carefully navigated the descent of Omega Street, my mother semi-conscious. Occasionally she opened her eyes, and murmured, "Fred." Darkness followed them down the hill, the footing treacherous, the drifts to his thighs. He couldn't make out the houses. Not a single automobile abroad. When he reached the barber shop, he halted. He had no feeling in his fingers, my mother, heavier with each tread, slipping from his arms. He refused to let go of the bread and the rum cake. He had to rest a moment, but he dared not put my mother down. He had to get her home. Once over the Hoeveler Street Bridge, they could take refuge a moment in the bakery. He slid and fell to a knee – my mother moaned – willed himself up, and peered across the bridge. Stagno's light was extinguished.

My father gathered my mother closer and staggered onto the bridge deck and headed home, over roads taken and otherwise – through all the fictions, including my own, in which we were snared – until those roads and my parents faded.

In the end, we remember our lives exclusive of the truth – which doesn't make us liars. But what does it make us? Federico Schiaretta's cobbler shop had been ancient, dry as bones, the wiring improvised and primitive. Perhaps a forgotten, seething De Nobili? A certain sinister element that infested East Liberty? Federico was a racketeer. That had never been a secret. Perhaps something else entirely. A lethal volt of ire on a day Federico was galled? Spontaneous combustion? The *malocchio*: the evil eye, a curse? My grandfather's building was not the first in East Liberty to have mysteriously taken fire.

We invent what only the dead alone have witnessed

and understood. While the ghosts of East Liberty consorted at will with the living, they were barred from testimony. In the end, what really happened doesn't matter. The real truth, more imaginative, more unbelievable than falsehood, remains the carnage of the past.

So, alone, without Fred, the dog, for solace, I waited and prayed – as I had waited and prayed all of my life – for Travis and Rita Sweeney to barge from that impenetrable pall of snow through the kitchen door.

INFESTATION

On a frigid night, in the last few days of December, Fritz and Claire drive downtown to see the Pittsburgh premier of *The Exorcist* at The Warner.

Claire has read the novel, a best-selling paperback with a distorted face that looks like the pistil and vulvaform stigma of a purple orchid smeared on its cover. She insists Fritz read it, but he refuses. He doesn't want his vision of the devil in any way complicated. He prefers a cartoon abstraction: a man in a red devil suit, with a Van Dyke and trident. An image he can easily dismiss. The devil who lives in the novel, however, the real Devil, Claire assures him, is the seductive, cloaked wayfarer, that most exquisite and alluring of all angels, Lucifer, who presented himself to Jesus in the desert, who can molt volcanic rock into bread or convince a devout man to slide a razor across his windpipe. Not a metaphor or a symbol – but an extant demon.

The movie is interrupted repeatedly because viewers break down or faint. A woman suffers a massive stroke and has to be rushed to the hospital by paramedics. A somnolent weeping pervades the theatre. Many simply walk out. Claire squeezes Fritz's hand between both of hers and emits a static crackle each time she gasps. After Regan, the little possessed girl, played carnally by kewpie-like Linda Blair, drives a crucifix into her vagina, Fritz veils his eyes with his free hand and scans the remainder of the movie through his fingers.

The film concludes with a close-up of the little girl, drained and seared, the bloody tatters of deliverance, yet clearly beatified by the exorcism that results in the deaths of two Jesuits. Yet, as Mike Oldfield's score, *Tubular Bells*, a diabolical *Panis Angelicus*, filters through the catatonic theatre, there is the unmistakable sense that the demon has not at all been vanquished but loosed once and for all. Then the audience files, like the condemned on their way to the death house, into the crystalline last days of 1973 – so dazzlingly cold that the famous clock depended from Kaufmann's department store expires.

Later, in Claire's apartment, where Fritz often spends the night, she explains that possession starts with *infestation* – the first manifestations of the demon. In the movie, the first sign of infestation comes from the attic, what Regan's mother assumes are skittering rats. Half the time, Claire says, she thinks she's possessed. Like rats are racing along the joists in her brain, diving into her bloodstream, gnawing on the wires that splice her together. There are entire rooms within Claire occupied by rats. They have offices where they talk on telephones and take down information to file in their long, grey cabinets. They are planning something. Fritz and Claire laugh at this. But Fritz wants her to drop it. Since they left the movie, he's been hearing things: a scat across a washboard, a stick dragged along an alley floor.

Claire sighs, smiles, and slips out of her sweater, stands there, protractedly unbuttoning her blouse, shirttails hanging over the front of her jeans. She unzips them, but so tight, they remain glued to her hips.

She walks to Fritz on the couch and puts her hands on his shoulders. He slips his thumbs in her belt loops and tugs the jeans down her unshaved legs until she walks out of them and sits next to him.

They smoke a joint and end up in bed, a mattress on the floor, surrounded by candles, incense, the music of Ravi Shankar. Fritz cannot stop thinking about the movie, the guttural voice of Regan as she blasphemes. He realizes he's been hearing that voice all his life, but he can't place it. He shouldn't have seen the movie. He shouldn't have smoked the reefer.

Claire says again there's something inside her, and smiles. "I'm possessed," she says. Fritz wants her to stop talking about possession. He doesn't like the smile.

"Let's call upon our dead ancestors," she suggests.

And indeed they are snared, on the mattress, in a séance ring of candles, the sitar music taking them farther and farther away from Claire's tidy apartment on Jackson Street, not terribly far from where Fritz lives with his mother and father. Fritz's mother's father, Federico, the cobbler, Fritz's namesake, died in the fire that destroyed his shop on Station Street. Fred the Shoemaker believed there were people born with the power to put the eyes on you, the *molocchhio.* Fred visited Grazziella, the Omega Street mage, to obtain roots and salves. He maintained shrines to the saints who wield the *pistolas* that kill devils.

Fritz's mother is just as superstitious as her father. Fritz refuses to summon Federico, yet afire, gone before Fritz ever met him. Fritz wishes him Godspeed and peace, but he doesn't want him or any of those Old World haunted *paesani* coming back, God forbid, from Mount Carmel Cemetery.

But Claire finds the company of the *morto* illuminating. She often converses with her dead grandmother.

She asks if Fritz can see the fog billowing through the apartment. "Often fog is an infestation." He thinks he sees it, wisping in the cornices, spreading along the floor.

Claire is so powerful that Fritz is having her hallucinations, too. But, of course, that can't be. He slips off the mattress, pulls on his jeans, steps outside the circle of candles, then walks into the dark bathroom for a glass of water. He turns on the light, sees himself. Dark hair getting long, his shadowy face. His eyes are clear, but he looks troubled. "It's okay," he says very softly.

Back in bed, he holds Claire tightly, runs his hands over her smooth body, kisses her forehead, breasts, and shoulders. Looks into her so deeply he sees the rats in their offices, scribbling, taking notes, typing away.

Fritz and Claire have been together nearly five months. He does not want to be without her, yet worries he will be with her forever. Fritz wants to escape Claire. She's insane – in the manner of his mother. But he loves Claire. He loves his mother. Perhaps he's possessed. Perhaps Claire – perhaps his mother – is the infestation.

He has sworn never to fall for an Italian – like his mother: with her sacramental devotion to getting back at people, making them pay for every wrong she catalogues and nurtures; her mouth that assassinates people, then closes against them, like the gates of Heaven, not a word nor prayer nor hand to help them out of the flames of Hell once she succumbs to vendetta; whatever she does at The Suicide King, the club she works at as a *hostess.* Fritz refuses to even walk down the street The King's on – the same street the Park Schenley's on, where his Irish father's a waiter – for fear of seeing his mother dangling from the ceiling in a go-go cage.

That torrent of Napolitano blood from his mother

gnaws at him like rats, that recessive speck of lunacy that filters capriciously through his veins. Claire's family is Calabrese – even worse. Her father is a beast, an *animale*, that kicks down doors and drags his prey out to the street.

Claire reads Fritz's mind. "Don't worry," she says. "I'm not your mother."

"I wasn't thinking about my mother." He turns and reaches for his cigarettes on the floor next to the mattress.

She smiles. "Come closer." He lights the cigarette. "Look at the Christmas tree." The tree is in the far corner of the room. Fritz set it up, and he and Claire spangled it with wildly-colored construction paper chains they'd both learned to make as first grade classmates all the way back at Saints Peter and Paul. He remembers Claire as a tiny, starving bird whose refusal to eat her lunch was a daily opera – the ravishing Sister Hyacinth draped above her with a raised stick. He had loathed Hyacinth – the way she terrorized Claire. But he had wanted to scream at Claire to pick up her sandwich and eat it – so he wouldn't have to listen to Hyacinth's sinister sing-song. Now he's hearing Hyacinth's voice oozing in his skull, and he realizes it's always been there – another infestation.

Yet, it also strikes him, at that very moment, that Claire, even as a six-year-old, so frail, as if about to deliquesce, fading into the ether by degrees each time Hyacinth's stick struck the table top, had the unimaginable will for her ritual ceremony with Hyacinth. Tiny Claire would not take her bulging white eyes from her untouched sandwich, would not speak, would not eat – no matter what, unto death, it seemed to Fritz back then.

As they gaze at the tree, it shimmies and glows, though it is not strung with lights. This goes on a moment or two. Fritz looks away, and, when he returns his eyes to the tree, it sits there utterly still. It is easy to rationalize the tree's sudden animation. Claire's apartment is on the second floor of an enormous, drafty old house – though Claire has cautioned that a sudden inexplicable draft is often an infestation.

As they stare at the Christmas tree, Claire whispers: "Frederick," his Christian name, which she calls him exclusively. "Do you hear that?"

The vaguest scuff of boots on the vestibule stairs leading up to Claire's apartment. Compton, Claire's old boyfriend, dressed wholly in black, come to exact revenge. But he's locked up. In the summer, he bashed out the windows in Claire's car. He threatened to set her apartment on fire, to kill Fritz. He must have gotten out of jail. He's come to kill them both. Compton is the devil.

Barefoot, in just jeans, Fritz gets up, goes to Claire's door, opens it and peers down the long stairs. He walks down to the vestibule, steps out on the porch, and smokes a cigarette. The big houses and the street are silent. The sky is an immaculate black plate of steel and ice. It is the portal off the earth, and tonight there is nothing to keep Fritz from being sucked up by it. He flicks the orange butt into the street and hurries inside.

Claire has wrapped up in a shawl and sits on the mattress. She wears a dripping black lace mantilla that Catholic girls wear to church: that demure, contemplative, untouchable innocence vouchsafed in stained glass and first communion commemoratives.

There in the sanctuary, at Saints Peter and Paul, staring at those girls, as a second-grade communicant – Claire, his classmate, among them – Fritz started thinking of the devil, but not with anything like the certitude of the word, *devil*, or even *flesh*, but with more of a vague indeterminate anxiety. Now he hears it again: a clicking, the sound of sin – the way it eats into your soul, imperceptibly at first, and then one day you're doomed. The infestation of impure thoughts – those girls he learned to long for in church.

Long before Claire read the book or saw the movie, she had studied demon possession. Documented cases abound. The Catholic Church corroborates every bit of it. Even as Fritz and Claire sit there, in Claire's apartment, possessed people check into Saint Francis, Mayview, Western Psych. Every crazy house in Pittsburgh overflows with them.

Claire pulls the novel from somewhere behind her and holds it in front of Fritz. Purple, vibrating, it rests on her open palm a foot from his face. "I've seen it levitate," she says, then that smile.

Fritz snatches the book from her hand, dashes to a window, and flings it to the frigid night. She continues to smile, stands, and drops the shawl, naked – forbiddingly beautiful – save for the mantilla. "I want you to perform an exorcism on me."

Fritz envisions her trussed to the mattress, shape-shifting, grunting filthy epithets, as he rains holy water upon her. He is close to blacking out.

What hangs in abeyance this night is the struggle between good and evil: Jesus wandering the desert, strung out from forty days and forty nights of fasting, while that son-of-a-bitch necromancer flatters Him, coaxes Him to leap from the church steeple. That same devil who haunts East Liberty – the Italian neighborhood where Fritz and Claire were born and grew up – seducing little boys to jump off the Meadow Street Bridge: the first warm flush once the syringe depresses into their arteries. Claire comes from a long line of vicious men – her father and brothers, Compton. Satan is the logical heir of that patrimony.

If Fritz stays with Claire, in her apartment, he is in peril – even deadly peril. If he walks out, he'll be delivered. He will have chosen light over darkness, life over death. But, tonight, he doesn't want to lose her. That will happen soon enough. He sees it now: a day when he'll call and she'll be gone – the line disconnected, the apartment emptied – to a monastery or convent. On her kitchen table is a large manila envelope from The Sisters of Mercy in Erie. She's told him, more than once, she'd like to be martyred.

The young, tortured Jesuit in the movie, Father Karras, his faith dwindled, demands the devil take him, forsake the little possessed girl. Just behind Fritz's eyes, that scene plays over and over: the demon divulging from Regan into Karras, the priest's face greening, capillaries firing, eyes milky. Father Karras flings himself to his death – through the window pane, thudding down that long medieval stone staircase in Georgetown.

Fritz's vision narrows – smoldering, blackening, at its edges. In the shrinking lens stands Claire, cradling the cat that Compton, in one of his furies, tried to murder. Fritz does not like the cat, but pretends to. He can't even pronounce her name: *Cassiopeia.* From Claire's breasts, the cat stares at him with green glowing eyes.

"Frederick," whispers Claire.

The sitar music grates and whines – so heavenly, it is demonic. Fritz is about to rip the record from the turntable when it simply ceases. Then rumbling, the entire house shaking, as the furnace engages, then the whistle and thunder of the ductwork. Salt trucks, down in the street, shudder, chains peeling, slag and rock salt eating at the ice.

"Frederick," she says again. She holds now, instead of Cassiopeia, a crystal cruet of holy water blessed by

Pope John XXIII. On its face is a crucifix.

It is imperative that Fritz leave Claire's apartment. Soon her head will swivel 360 degrees. She'll profane in a guttural rusted brogue. Her father will tear the door from its hinges and scatter Fritz in pieces. Compton will appear with a knife.

But: the sound, in her mouth, of the name given him at Baptism. Her body. How can Fritz abandon her?

Hosanna

On our front stoop – a block of concrete wrapped in a rusting scroll of wrought iron – my parents hold hands in the peeling green and white glider the previous tenants left. I'm at their feet on the steps, clutching stalks of Easter palm I've brought home from early Palm Sunday Mass. In the oven are hot cross buns my father has whipped up from memory. He's a good cook – my mother doesn't cook at all – and not a bad baker. But he's never confected anything so powerful, so invested with immortality, as hot cross buns.

My mother wants my father to go to church with her and renew their wedding vows. They were married on Larimer Avenue by a crooked alderman named Vince Mercurio. My mother was pregnant with me. Now she worries that without the sanctifying imprimatur of the church their union remains unconsecrated and, therefore, I will always be a bastard.

My father smiles and nods, as if agreeing with my mother. To disagree would trigger an argument. It is a beautiful Sunday morning, and my mother wears a pretty pink dress. Her hair is still damp from the shower, unadorned, silky pale yellow in the fractals of sunlight dusting the porch. She is happy, and neither my father nor I want to break the spell.

"It would be really nice. Don't you think, Travis?"

she says to my dad. Then she lifts his hand, clamped in hers, and kisses it.

"It would be a memorable occasion, Rita."

"It's important to me."

"Then it's important to me."

"Matrimony is a sacrament."

"Yes."

"You're not listening to a word I'm saying. Are you, Travis?"

"Matrimony is a sacrament, Rita. Of course, I'm listening."

"Fritz could be the ring bearer. I'd like a ring this time."

With his silver lighter, my father lights my mother's cigarette, then his own. He pours tomato juice into his beer, then heavily peppers it from the shaker on the milk box they use for a table. My mother drinks a Bloody Mary. He clamps the cigarette between his lips, slips a piece of palm from my hand and begins to fold and braid it. Smoke leaks from the corners of his stubbled mouth and slides from his long nose.

My parents were both raised in the Catholic Church before the Ecumenical Council, but they long ago fell away. They don't even observe Easter duty. I've received the sacraments and go to Catholic school. Every Sunday, as they sleep off their Saturday nights, often into the afternoon – my dad's a waiter down the street from the club where my mother hostesses – I attend Mass alone. I pray for their souls, but I feel myself falling away, too.

My mother is excommunicated, disowned by God, disowned by her family – for refusing to marry in the church, for conceiving a baby outside of Holy Matrimony – and this has branded her like a scarified harlot. Her belief is styled to suit her: curses; incantations;

the evil eye, *malocchio*; visits to the neighborhood *strega*, Grazziella, for love potions and fertility rituals. Now, the second baby she so desperately wants to conceive will not nest in her womb, and she realizes it is time to make peace with God.

My father claims she's a pagan. He says this with affection, but my mother takes it as an insult. More than anything, she believes in vendetta and frets that God will call her to answer for everything. Her barrenness is merely the beginning of the punishment she expects. If the cautions and predictions are true, if the writ that she has ignored and flaunted is indeed the word of God, as she was taught, then she's in trouble. My father, excommunicated too, for the same offenses as his wife, doesn't believe in any of it. He'll be content with whatever turns out to be the ultimate upshot. It could go either way. Eternity is not something that concerns my father. He understands perfectly the risks.

"We could take a trip," my mother says. "Like a honeymoon." Cigarette poised an inch away from her pale lips, so innocent and untouched without lipstick, she stares straight up at small, powdery clouds sighing across the blue sky. Smoke from her mouth lifts into the clouds. Her exposed neck is white and soft.

"We could take a trip," echoes my father.

"Remember the first trip?"

"With clarity, Rita."

My mother and father conceived me on a vibrating bed in a Braxton County, West Virginia, motel. Next to the Elk River in a Christmas Eve blizzard – after they got lost on their way to the ocean – and their car froze up.

My mother lowers her face from the clouds. She is smiling. She leans towards my father and kisses his cheek. The way he looks at her – she has made him so happy with this kiss. My father returns the palm to me in the shape of a cross.

"Where did you learn to do that?" asks my mother, staring at the cross.

"I was an altar boy."

"I don't believe it. I've never seen you make anything."

"I can make crosses. I think I even wanted to be a priest. For the longest time, I had faith."

My dad is now looking at those same dreamy clouds my mother has invested with her smoke. He releases a big drag, and it jets up and joins my mother's.

"Then you met me," my mother prompts.

"Then I met you."

"And lost your faith."

"Surrendered it."

"You lost your faith."

"I didn't say that, Rita. I never said I no longer had faith."

"But that's what you meant.

"It isn't at all what I meant. You're worth my immortal soul, Rita. I knew you'd get me in trouble with God when I met you."

This is a moment of impasse. Things might swing either way. They could pull switchblades or begin right there, in front of me, tearing at each other with theatrical longing. I clutch the palm cross my father made me – so perfect as to be miraculous. It vibrates in my hand. With it, I could raise the dead. It's the only thing my father, a waiter, has ever made for me other than food. He does not own tools or drive a car. But he knows how to make a cross.

My parents look at me. Their love lifts me up into the clouds they've chuffed out of their mouths. The smell of hot cross buns baking in the oven – at the very moment they are perfected – gives me the power to read their minds. They have decided not to fight. They will remain my parents.

"I actually had a vision once," says my father. "You and I were at the altar at Saints Peter and Paul's, and about us was a band of angels, and Jesus himself pronounced us man and wife, and all the people we love had come back to life. They filled the church, and, when we walked down the aisle, they sang 'Holy God.'"

My mother looks at my father. She doesn't know if he's serious. He's both. Believes none of it. Believes with all his heart and soul.

"I had that same vision too," she says.

My dad takes her in his arms. "We're a couple of mystics, Rita." He kisses her. Her hair is perfectly blonde, not a speck of the black spill – her true color – that habitually clings to her part. Today, in the sunlight, her eyebrows are blonde too, her skin a milky pink. She is soft as Mary. It's the cross my father has made. It has begun to exert its dominion over everything.

"Then, will you stand on the altar at Saints Peter and Paul and have Father Guisina pronounce us man and wife?"

My father stares at her, struck by her transformation. She gleams like Mount Sinai.

"I will, Rita, so help me God."

My mother's incomparable beautiful brown eyes fill with tears.

"I'll place gardenias in your hair, Rita. We'll invite the dead."

They kiss, then stare at me again. I feel in my veins the glorious insanity of their commingled blood.

"If you'll excuse me, Beautiful," my father says and kisses her again. Then he rises. "Fritzy, keep an eye on your mother. I'll be right back."

My mother pats the spot on the glider my father has vacated. I sit next to her. She puts her arm around me.

"Your father and I are going to get married in the church."

I look at her and nod. When she's like this, bewitched by something, like this idea of her and my father as bride and groom, so happy, even though it can't last, I agree with her – no matter what.

"You'll wear a white linen suit with a bright red rose boutonnière, and you'll carry the ring on a white lace pillow."

I see myself, like Lazarus, in his resurrection suit, walking up the aisle behind my mother and father. Blazing through the Communion of Saints, pressed in stained glass like desiccated lilies, the sun streams down upon me. The ring glows like the Grail. Like science fiction. The organ pipes the wedding march. Father Guisina, senescent, palsied, shivers on the altar beneath the Crucifix. He wears long johns in August. Gray as the chancel walls, he dreams of the Stigmata.

My father returns with another Bloody Mary for my mother and a platter of hot cross buns. Currants and candied citrus break their gold, glistening surfaces emblazoned with white icing crosses. He gives her the drink and sets the platter down on the milk box, picks up a bun and breaks it. Incense wafts from the halves. He hands a half to my mother and recites: *"Half for you and half for me. Between us two shall goodwill be."* He crowds onto the glider on the other side of her and replenishes his drink. My mother looks at him quizzically. She holds the pastry. The transverse beam and the headboard of the cross melt into her open palm.

"Will we really get married in church, Travis?"

"I'm not opposed to the idea."

"I would bow my head," whispers my mother. "I would wear something pretty."

"Then we'll go to The Embers for lobster and champagne," declares my dad.

They turn to each other and laugh; they kiss, clink their glasses together and drink deeply. They bite into the buns and drink again.

Waving palm fronds, people on their way home from High Mass stream by our house. We know them, and they know us – from the neighborhood all these years and years – back to when my Irish father from Larimer Avenue was an altar boy at Saints Peter and Paul and put the paten to the *Napolitano* throat of Rita Schiaretta, his future wife, as she knelt at the communion rail and awaited the host. Before they found each other, before they lay down together on that vibrating bed in West Virginia, before their spurious vows in slick Vince's dingy Larimer Avenue office.

"These are so delicious, Travis," says my mother. She picks up a bun and offers it to me. "Here, Fritzy. While it's still hot."

"I can't," I say.

"Of course, you can, Honey. They're scrumptious. It'll melt in your mouth." She holds the bun to my lips. "Take a bite."

"I can't, Mom."

"Why not?"

"I gave up sweets. For Lent."

"You can have one little bite. It won't hurt a thing."

My mother is still smiling. Nothing bad has yet happened. I know what to do, what not to do, to keep her smiling, to preserve this lovely sunny Sabbath. The bun is fixed at my closed mouth. It smells heavenly. I feel its warmth. At the other end of the glider, my father waits, sipping his beer and tomato juice, smoking his cigarette.

"I made a promise to God, Mom."

"Those son-of-a-bitch nuns put that in your head." Her smile has gone to the bad. "Eat this goddam thing, Fritzy."

"Rita," my father interjects. "What are you doing?"

"What if I paid you to eat it?"

"Jesus Christ, Rita."

"I'll hand you a ten-dollar bill if you take a bite of this."

I shift my eyes from the white cross in my face to my mother's big brown eyes. They yearn deeply for something, it seems, I can supply only by eating the hot cross bun. Beyond that yearning, however, locked behind the ornate, carven vaults of her gorgeous irises, coils an even greater desire. The devil, with his bag of dope, has hold of her. He's already got her tied off. The vein throbs indecently in her white arm, her pink dress. In spins the needle. Down goes the plunger. Back roll her eyes.

If only she would swear to my father and me that it is the devil. When we ask, "Rita, Honey, what is it?" "Mom, what's wrong?" If she would explain, then we'd know what it is, and we could endure this opera she's authored into the morning – that could blow over in minutes, or last like a solemn liturgy the duration of Holy Week. Perhaps until Pentecost.

"Eat it," she commands.

"Mom, I can't do it."

My mother bolts out of the glider and throws the bun into the street. Her Bloody Mary laps over the rim of its glass and spills a few drops on her pink dress. She drops back into the glider, stares catatonically at her dress, the egg-shaped tiny red droplets that punctuate her lap. "Oh my God," she whispers, easing the drink onto the milk box. "Oh my God."

"Rita, what is it?" asks my father.

She has the hem of the dress in her hands.

"Look at my dress," she says.

"It's beautiful," replies my dad. "Those little dabs of red. Like they belong there."

"It's bad luck."

"Rita, everything is not bad luck. You spilled your drink."

"I've sinned, Travis."

"Rita, please. This is not about sin."

"God's punishing me."

Our neighbors, our friends, caper along the street. But it's like we're not even here. As if we're sinners, they don't even look at us. The children sing *Hosanna* – what Jesus's executioners shouted when he rode a colt into Jerusalem on the first Palm Sunday.

My father stands and tries to put his arms around my mother, but she gets to her feet and backs away. "Rita. Let's walk over to the church right now and get married."

"I'm not going to kiss some priest's ass, Travis. What would some priest know about bad luck? What could that dried-up old greenhorn tell me about the sacrament of Holy Matrimony?"

My father turns his head away from my mother and scripts out a long sentence of smoke. He does not smile, like he usually tries to do when my mother, mainlined on bad luck and vendetta, inches out of our lives like this. He is not angry. He simply does not know what to do. "Probably not a goddamn thing, Rita," he finally says.

Still backing, barefoot, down the concrete steps of our little stoop, stained dress clutched in her fists, like a net in which she'll harvest her punishment, my mother asks, "Fritzy, what do you think?"

She is turning away now – to join the procession. My father hurries toward her, his hands extended.

"They killed Him," I answer.

The Pall Bearer

I'm at 5th and Negley, thumbing towards East Liberty, when a smoky blue Cadillac, a Sedan deVille with tinted windows, glides to the curb, and the back door swings open.

The guy in the back says, "Get in the car," moves over, and pats the seat he's just vacated. He wears a suit and tie, a gangster hairdo. His lips twist around a cigarette. He's what my mother calls a *gavone*. I have two impulses at once: do exactly as he's commanded and slide in or run like hell. Then he says again, "Get in the car."

Suddenly, the front passenger window zips down and the guy riding shotgun says, "Jump in, Fritzy." It's my dad, also in a suit, smiling. The guy in the back, the *gavone*, smiles, too. Like the whole thing is a joke.

I get in the car. Jimmy, the dishwasher at the Park Schenley, the high-dollar restaurant where my dad waits tables, mans the wheel – in a suit. I'm on my way home from school, at Saint Sebastian's, where it's required you wear a coat and tie every day, so I'm dressed up, too.

The four of us in this Caddy on a Thursday afternoon on a pretty fall day. But doing what? Why is my dad in the car when usually he'd be punched in at work? I hadn't been aware that he even owned a suit. I've never seen him look so sharp. And what's with Jimmy? Why isn't he sweating his ass off, dish-dogging at the slop sink, in the Park Schenley kitchen? And whose boat? You don't drive a Caddy on a dish-dog's hourly. And the guy I'm sitting next to. Who the heck is he?

My dad turns and says, "Fritz, this is Wee Russo."

I turn to Wee. He holds out his big, fat hand and says, "Pleased to meet you, Fritz."

As we shake hands, I say: "How are you? Nice to meet you." He makes a big deal of squeezing my hand and looking piercingly into my eyes, his face tilted theatrically.

"And you know Jimmy," says my dad.

"Yes. Hi, Jimmy." Jimmy's been to our house.

Jimmy says, "Hello, Brother Fritz." He wears sunglasses and bobs his head to an 8-track of Ahmad Jamal: piano, strings in the background, the occasional *ratta-tat-tat* of the skins, mellow, but picking up momentum. The interior of the car is the exact color of its exterior – smoky, subversive. The seats are plush, velour. I've never been in a Cadillac.

Strange as it is to encounter my dad like this – though he seems not at all taken aback by the fact that we're in this luxurious automobile together on an afternoon when he's supposed to be somewhere else – I'm grateful he's here. My dad would never characterize himself as a brave man, and my mother taunts him about his lack of courage, but I'm not afraid of Wee Russo with my dad in the car, and having Jimmy behind the wheel is comforting.

The Caddy has a telephone in a little box between the front seats, and a safe, and a bar, too. The three of them drink Crown Royal as we cruise north on Negley Avenue. On the dashboard stands a white statue of Jesus, His flaming pierced heart scarlet.

Every few minutes, the phone rings. Wee Russo answers it and writes down numbers on a pocket spiral notebook. He keeps his conversations coded. I don't care about what he's doing – taking action, making book on the looming football weekend. The Steelers are starting to win. Bitter fans are coming back around.

"Fritz," my father says, turning to look at me, "we're on our way to a funeral and later to Wee's club."

"How was school today, Fritz?" asks Wee.

"It was fine, Mr. Russo."

The phone rings.

"Excuse me," Wee says.

My mother's voice leaks through the phone: "Wee, I'd like to speak to Travis."

My dad takes the phone and explains the plan: he'll see her at the cemetery, then see what's what after the funeral, maybe drop by Wee's joint. My mother is supposed to be at The Suicide King, where she hostesses, not far from my dad's job. But she's on the phone with my dad, saying, "Yes, Travis" and "Okay, Travis," she'll meet him and Jimmy and Wee at the cemetery. They keep talking about the funeral, but a church is never mentioned, nor any mention of the deceased. My dad doesn't tell her I'm in the car – a secret I instinctively know I must keep, though there's nothing more catastrophic than keeping a secret from my mother. Now I'm wondering why she has the number to this Caddy and how she fits in to whatever's going down. It's clear she knows Wee Russo.

After they hang up, Wee asks: "You play ball?

"Not really."

"Fritz is on the wrestling team at Saint Sebastian's," says my dad.

"Good," said Wee. "You got to know how to protect yourself."

"But the books come first," says Jimmy.

"The broads come first," counters Wee. The phone rings and, again, he says, "Excuse me."

This time, it's action. Wee gives the lines, then records everything in his little notebook. Jimmy dangles his empty Dixie cup toward the back seat without moving his eyes from the road. We're on Lincoln Avenue now, cruising by the mortuary where Ethel Waters starred in that episode of *Route 66*. Wee lifts the Crown Royal from the bar, slips it from its purple shroud, and pours Jimmy a righteous jolt. Jimmy in his gold suit, digging Jamal.

"Splash for me too, please, Wee," says my dad, and holds out his cup. Wee pours the same for my dad. "I'm sorry we don't have anything for you, Fritz."

"He's old enough for a little taste," says Wee.

"No, he's not," says my dad.

"Rita'd break your jaw, Travis, and worse for you, Wee," says Jimmy.

Wee and my dad laugh.

"Rita doesn't like me," says Wee.

"That's not true, Wee," says my dad.

"Rita don't take no shit," Jimmy says. I've heard my mother refer to Jimmy as a *hophead*.

"No, she doesn't," says my dad.

The phone rings. Wee just listens and then says, "Okay, I'll tell them." He hangs up and says, "D'Genovese says we need another pallbearer."

"We have, Fritz," says my dad.

"There it is," says Jimmy.

"Okay," says Wee.

Then my dad says: "Wee just opened a discotheque, Fritz."

"On Centre Avenue," Wee says. He whips out a silver business card embossed with glossy red script – *The Wee Room* – then, with a fancy pen, scribbles on the back of the card, and hands it to me. "Lifetime membership," he says, pleased with himself. Very slick.

"That's a nice gift, Wee," says my dad. "Something Fritz can put into play once he turns twenty-one."

"Twenty-one?" says Wee.

"Twenty-one," says my dad.

"You serious?"

"I am, Wee. This is my son."

"He's a good boy," says Wee, and pats my arm. "But I hope he doesn't wait until he's twenty-one – for anything."

We're on our way to Mount Carmel Cemetery, the *campo Santo,* where the Italian dead of East Liberty – having forsaken the streets and alleys they walked during their corporeal lives – have reassembled the neighborhood beneath rows of tombstones. I'm going to be a pallbearer at an unnamed person's funeral. I'm in this Cadillac, and my dad is acting like a kingpin: Humphrey Bogart, in a midnight blue suit, shockingly white shirt, California Satins necktie, blue eyes and black hair – something else, too smooth. Soon my mother will join us, and everything will shift – but how?

We proceed up Lincoln. Wee takes a little action on the phone. Jimmy sways behind the wheel. My dad smokes, sips Crown Royal, and moons classically out the window as we pass Joe Westray's Ebony Lounge. It's a pretty day. Glorious sun, turquoise sky, leaves still on some of the trees. Black guys – with processes and mustaches, sandals, trilbies and flat caps – sit in kitchen chairs on the sidewalk, smoking and drinking. They are about to reveal something. The front door is wide open – dark inside, flashes of light, the World Series on the black-and-white TV behind the bar. Next door to the Ebony Lounge is the Church of Corpus Christi.

Crowning Cemetery Hill is St. Joseph's Military School, where bad boys are sent to labor for the nuns. The last streetcar stop is up here, the end of the line.

Jimmy glides through a hairpin – suddenly, spread beneath us glitter the graves of Mount Carmel – then through the main entrance to the chapel and noses up to D'Genovese's hearse, parked behind my mother's Impala. The casket is visible through the hearse's rear window. A tiny, stooped man in a suit gets out of the hearse and walks to the Caddy. Jimmy push-buttons down his window.

"Whatta you say, Jimmy?" says this man and shoves his little hand – a star sapphire on his pinky – into the car. He's old – a big, gray mustache and a shiny brown toupee. His purple arm band says *D'Genovese Mortuary*.

"Whatta you say, John?" says Jimmy.

"It's always a hell of a thing," says John. Only a few inches taller than the car, he peers into the interior and smiles. "Hello, gents. Deepest sympathy."

Everybody says hello to John. My dad nods at me and says, "This is my son, Fritz, John. Fritz, this is John D'Genovese, an old friend."

"Pleased to meet you, Fritz," says D'Genovese. He reaches into the back seat, and we shake hands.

"Good to meet you, Mr. D'Genovese," I say.

"Looks just like Rita," he says.

"No luck with the priests?" asks Wee.

"Nah, they wouldn't touch it with a ten-foot pole."

"Sons of bitches," says Wee.

"We'll be okay," says D'Genovese. "I squared it with the cemetery. They'll move him out of the chapel and get him in the ground. If the shit hits the fan, I'll go to the bishop. He owes me more than one favor."

"Thanks, John," says my dad.

D'Genovese splays out his palms as if in supplication. "My pleasure. We're all on the same conveyor belt. Poor Cuss. So many bad breaks. He was never right after the war." He reaches inside his suit and pulls out a silver cigarette case, puts a cigarette in his mouth and lights it with a chrome Zippo. Then he surveys the inside of the Caddy again and says, "There's only four of you, and I had to give up lifting coffins twenty years ago. I haven't driven a hearse in forty, but I want this all hush-hush. Just between us." He peers at me as he mouths those last three words.

My dad looks at him and says, "Absolutely, John. Just between us."

Out across the white stones in sunlight wanders my mother, smoking a cigarette, in a plain black dress; black hat, veiled over one eye; black stockings and high heels. Rita Sweeney. Rita Schiaretta Sweeney. Behind her, in the towering distance, looms a black crucifix. Its ivory Christ watches over His vast acreage of Italians.

"Here comes Rita," says my dad. "She'll be a pall-bearer."

"Women can't be pallbearers," D'Genovese says.

My mother floats across Mount Carmel. She doesn't know I'm here.

"We're talking about Rita," says my dad. "She makes five."

"Five's plenty," says Wee. "Rita can lift like two people."

"Good enough," says D'Genovese. "God won't mind."

"Neither will Cuss," says Jimmy.

I get out of the car and walk toward my mother. She lifts a hand to shield the sun and, as we get closer, she drops the hand and smiles in a way I've never seen her smile before – as if she's happy. She doesn't even ask what I'm doing here. She could make a scene, climb all over my dad – *What the hell is this? Fritzy showing up at Cuss's funeral and you don't tell me?* – not speak to us for a month. But she strolls over, puts her arm around me –

I'm almost taller than she is – gives me a nice kiss, then takes my arm, something she's never done, and says: "I was looking for my father's grave, but I couldn't find it."

I hadn't wanted to know the identity of the dead guy. I'd been content to carry the coffin into the chapel, pray, whatever, commend this anonymous stiff to the best hereafter he could expect – the unrelieved glare of *perpetual light* – and then see what happened next. But now I know it's Cuss and everything caves in a little. Jimmy, my dad, and Cuss – another waiter at the Park Schenley – worked together. I'm already using past tense. I don't want it to be Cuss. I don't want it to be anybody. I'm satisfied with the way things have gone so far: the Caddy ride with my dad and Wee and Jimmy, all the mystery surrounding the dead guy, my mother somehow in the mix. I want it to end right now, with my mother dolled up like this, her arm looped through mine; my dad, in that boss suit, walking out of the sun toward us, smiling, my mother smiling back at him.

Then my dad reaches us. He and my mother kiss, look into each other's eyes, and smile. With her free hand, my mother takes my father's arm. Here we are, the three of us, as we've never been before, in our good clothes, at Mount Carmel Cemetery, on the most achingly beautiful, brittle autumn day I've ever witnessed: my mother between my father and me, her hands threaded through our arms.

"It's Cuss," I say.

My mother looks away.

My father says: "It is."

The first time my father told me Cuss was an alien, I might have been around seven, maybe eight. My father had recently turned me on to Marvel Comics. They hooked me on the shadow realm, a clandestine chamber just on the other side of the wall, our wall –

where aliens abide. We live in a row-house duplex. I habitually catch the muted unrecognizable speech and rustlings of the neighbors but three inches away from where we eat and sleep and bathe. Aliens. Not necessarily creatures with otherworldly powers or freakish looks; but, rather, secret lives – lives too dangerous, too compromising, to share with others – lives like ours: mine and my mother's and father's.

"Cuss is an alien." No lead-in. No context. No Nothing. *Boom:* "Cuss is an alien." That's how my dad started the conversation.

My father has a sense of humor, and he's affectionate, but he's no kidder. Not the type to make fun of you, hold you down and tickle you, or tell you he has your nose. Nor does he make up stories to scare you. And he doesn't lie. My mother lies and rarely misses an opportunity to contradict my father, but when he suddenly outed that outrageous proclamation that Cuss was an alien, she said nothing, but nodded in grave affirmation.

Cuss and my dad worked together, and they'd known each other since childhood. My mother too goes way back with Cuss. Same neighborhood, East Liberty, where we sat that day in our kitchen, eating bacon and eggs and Italian toast, when my dad first broached the subject. Late Sunday afternoon, the sky a smeared blackboard. Cuss was due to pop in any second. Often on Sundays, the only day my parents and Cuss could loaf, he stopped by.

"What do you mean, *alien*?" I asked. "Like from another planet?"

"I don't know exactly what I mean, Fritz. I hesitate to say from another planet, but could be."

"Like secret powers or something?"

"I've seen his mouth seal over, just sort of

disappear. There's his nose, and there's his chin, but no mouth. Watch him when he eats."

I pictured Cuss's rubbery mouth, waffling over his face as he throttled his meringue, the blubbering laugh after one of his juvenile jokes. Sometimes his mouth really did disappear, a fleshy gnashing graft under his nose. On his forearm was a supernumerary nipple, but he wasn't the only man in East Liberty that bore one.

"Have you ever seen him wear a coat?" my dad continued. "No matter what the weather? If he shows up today – I'll bet it's ten degrees out there, a blizzard on the way – he won't be wearing anything to keep warm. He's indifferent to temperature."

"And all he eats is sweets," my mother added. "Period. Am I right, Travis?"

"As rain."

My mother's corroboration worried me. By then she would have told my father he was full of shit. *Bullshit, Travis,* she would have said. *You're such a bullshitter.* Not that day. They were in absolute deadpan agreement that Cuss was an alien, a breed engendered by longing and falsehood, and I detected not the least bit of irony in their deliveries, no private joke, no weird symbolic shtick they often rehearsed with me as their audience.

How fitting that Cuss would rise up out of East Liberty, a place crawling with aliens – silent, mutated, fragmentary beings walking the streets day and night, gazes moored on the pavement, mumbling, praying, filthy, in the same threadbare thrift garments day after day despite the season, as if they'd accidentally stumbled through the secret portal on the other side of the wall and were unable to retrace their steps to escape what we mistakenly term the real world – what my mother calls the cruel world.

Marooned, their time among the rest of us short,

but they have advice, if only we sidle close enough to hear their muttering, rather than suspiciously cross to the other side of the street when we see them amble our way: Rosie Noof-Noof, Iggy, Grazziella, Mooch, Platehead, Haggy, Montmorrissey Hilliard. They, too, are aliens. My mother drilled me to be afraid of them. But I've also been drilled to fight fear with scorn, to laugh in its face, to demean it. Then it hit me: my parents, Travis and Rita Sweeney – they had to be aliens. And what did that make me?

I decided that late Sabbath afternoon to study Cuss, make a little alien checklist in my head. He showed up around five. He never knocked and always came to the kitchen door. We were still at the table – my mom and dad, in robes and pajamas, sharing the same pack of Chesterfields, leisurely making the transition from coffee to booze.

I was merely a witness, happy to be in the smoky kitchen with my parents, still in the necktie I had worn to church hours ago, well before my parents made it out of bed. The doorknob turned: Cuss, framed in the curtain-less kitchen door window – a cameo of East Liberty woebegone. Sure enough, he was without a coat, snow and wind beating about him as he lurched into the kitchen, carrying a strawberry pie from Eat'N'Park. He looked a little like those deranged slavering Roman emperors in gladiator movies, who talk with mouthfuls of venison, wine spilling down their chins, but without the viciousness, an apologetic homely version, nothing whatsoever regal about him.

"Jesus, Cuss," said my mother. "Where's your coat?"

Cuss was dressed in his requisite white shirt and dark pants, saggy white socks and clerk shoes – his waiter outfit minus the bow tie and waistcoat.

"Who needs a coat," he said and then cracked up.

He lifted a finger, his salutary gesture before delivering one of his pathetic dirty jokes, and said: "Have I told you about the lady who goes into the hardware store to buy a screw?"

"Yeah, Cuss, you've shared that one," said my dad. "A classic."

"How about the parrot who fell off his perch?"

"Yep," said my dad. "We've heard it."

"Too much, aren't they?" Then, as if he'd actually told the jokes and brought the house down, he went to pieces, shimmying and seizing, his mouth haywire, choking as if he'd swallowed his tongue.

Cuss sat – across from me – and said, "Hello, Fritzy." He set the box with the pie in it in front of me. "Look what I brought you. Your favorite."

"Thanks, Cuss," I answered. But I didn't know what he was talking about.

"I got another hardware store joke," announced Cuss.

"We've heard it," said my dad.

"I swear to God, you haven't heard this one, Travis."

"We've heard it, Cuss."

"No, you haven't. Please let me tell it. I'll never tell another joke again if you let me tell it."

"Tell the joke," said my mother.

That made Cuss happy. He was already laughing – his mouth beginning to seal and graft, to disappear, but then it returned. "Okay," he said. "A lady walks into the hardware store and says she wants to buy a file. 'You want this little bastard?' the guy behind the counter asks. 'No,' she says. 'Gimme that big son of a bitch over there.'"

My mother and father laughed, which really pleased Cuss. He slapped his hands on his thighs and howled.

"Jesus Christ, Cuss," said my mother. "You're a regular jagoff. Let's cut that pie.

We ate the pie. Cuss spread sugar on his. He ate half of it. His mouth disappeared. I was three for three on the checklist: no coat, no mouth, and Cuss gorged on sweets.

When he left, my father hugged him. Cuss kissed my mother and handed me some change. Sometimes he laid an entire buck on me. I never thought of him as having a home or people, and I never asked where he went when he left our house. Like my father, he didn't drive. For the longest time, just because my dad had said so – and, because my mother did not refute him, did not smirk and wise-crack, but held her peace – I thought of Cuss as an alien.

But, of course, Cuss wasn't an alien. His mouth didn't really disappear. And perhaps he'd become impervious to cold because of his habitual exposure to it – maybe he couldn't afford a coat – and why begrudge someone sugar if that's his sole comfort. Who the hell knows? Cuss was what people call a *ciuccio,* a donkey, an ass. His affliction, that which made him alien, was supreme discomfort with being on this inhospitable earth. He just had a little secret. Not that different than the rest of us.

In the past many months, he'd stopped coming around. He'd been fired from the Park Schenley. My dad said he'd "gotten careless" – which might have meant anything from theft to drunkenness to brawling. He'd been hired to barkeep at The Pink Slip, a few blocks from Wee's discotheque, a joint notorious for sleaze and serving kids.

All I know is that – whatever happened to Cuss, whatever killed him – the church refused to bury him. No priest would preside. No real funeral. D'Genovese

– another guy from the neighborhood my mother and father and the others went way back with, who had become a mortician in prison, which seemed appropriate – made all the arrangements gratis and, through his connections, fixed things with the cemetery, and ensured Cuss's interment among the Mount Carmel *paesani*. I'm glad the casket is closed. Fourteen years old, and I've never glimpsed a corpse.

My mother and father and I walk toward the hearse, around which everyone clusters. My mother kisses Wee and Jimmy and D'Genovese. D'Genovese hands the five of us pairs of gray gloves. My mother and father pull theirs on with the others. Mine fit perfectly.

D'Genovese releases the giant hatch. The casket is silver, gleaming in the late afternoon sun. Leaves fall from the sycamores along the path to the chapel. Their trunks are white. The bark has scrolled away and lies curled on the ground.

D'Genovese grunts as he unmoors the casket and rolls it on casters inch by inch from the back of the hearse – my mother and father and I on one side, Wee and Jimmy on the other, as we assume the handles and heft Cuss into the chapel, where we lay him on a bier. D'Genovese trails with an American flag he spreads across the breast of the casket. There's an altar with a crucifix, behind which is a columbarium housing, in small, windowed receptacles, ornate cinerary urns with the ashes of the dead, their names – all of which I recognize – emblazoned on plaques: DiLampedusa, Leopardi, Pavese, Fante, Svevo, Moravia, Montale, Puzo, Giacometti, Calvino. It dawns on me that I don't know Cuss's real name.

No one recites the sacred writ or sings. There are no flowers. No symbolic knot of earth spread upon Cuss's casket. We take off our gloves and lay our palms on the flag-draped casket. In Wee's hand is a rosary. There is birdsong. The last of the sun floods the chapel.

Even when I thought Cuss was an alien, I was never afraid of him. I liked him pretty well. Maybe I loved him. When I was really little, he read me stories. One of the last times he visited, not all that long ago, he asked if I was too big for him to read to me. I had mistakenly thought he'd been kidding.

My father hands my mother his immaculate white handkerchief. She takes my arm again, and whispers, "Put all of this out of your mind, Fritzy."

Buon Anno

(for Roberto Clemente)

Keith needs the company, so I walk a few blocks to his parents' house, around 9:30, to play poker with him and his family – a New Year's Eve tradition at the Gentiles. It's a Sunday, the very last day of a leap year. The temperature is sixty degrees when normally, this time of year in Pittsburgh, it's more like six.

Keith flunked out of college and got his girl, Bonnie, pregnant. He and Bonnie have rented an apartment together on Penn Avenue over a flower shop. Bonnie's out with her friends for the evening. She works a few hours a week filing and answering the phone at Don Allen Chevrolet on Baum Boulevard. Keith hasn't found a job yet.

Keith's mother, who still has vestiges of exotic Napolitano beauty – thick, twisting tresses of black hair that hang to her shoulders – is devastated to the point that she refused to have a Christmas tree in the house this year. All the Gentiles have is the Nativity set on the coffee table in the living room, a few tiny red and green bulbs and tinsel stuffed into the barn along with Baby Jesus and his entourage. *Devastated:* the word she uses when she greets me at the door and kisses me on each cheek.

First, her son flunks out of school. All that money she and Mr. Gentile busted their asses to put back for his education down the toilet: he on the open hearth down at Mesta; she in the lunch room at Fulton School, and moonlighting, on her already destroyed legs until midnight four nights a week, deveining shrimp at Minutello's Restaurant. Then he gets this Bonnie, this *puttana* – the daughter of a couple of Calabrese greenhorns – pregnant; and now, on top of everything, they live together. They live in sin. She won't say it out loud, but that's what it is. They could have moved in with the Gentiles, at least until after the baby is born. What do they know about raising a child? They're babies themselves. And this Bonnie's parents can barely speak English. Shacking up – it had to be this girl's idea. Keith is a good boy, just a little too gullible.

Mrs. Gentile's trying to take it all in, not overreact, not throw gasoline on the fire. But, *Jesu Christe,* now what's Keith going to do? Shovel slag next to his father at Mesta? End up on dope like those *ciuccios* down on the corner? Exactly the things she and Mr. Gentile were trying to shield him from by sending him to college. His life is ruined. But first things first: Bonnie and Keith have to get married. Period. She wants to be a mother-in-law before a grandmother.

Under the best circumstances, Keith's mom is a little nuts, but not violent like my mother, or a screamer. But you wouldn't want to push her. Mrs. Gentile and my mom have known each other all their lives; they grew up together in this same neighborhood, East Liberty, went to Peabody High School together. They like each other. They pride themselves on taking no shit and saying exactly what's on their minds.

What Keith's parents don't know is that Bonnie's not pregnant at all. Three days ago, she had an abortion, something Keith blames himself for: a curse he wears on top of his electrified hair like broken glass.

Keith's plan is to tell his parents about the abortion before midnight signals the new year. He wants the whole thing out in the open, done with, assigned to 1972, a year he can check off as a giant ass-whipping, and then move into 1973 with a clean slate. Besides being superstitious – he wears around his neck one of those big chili pepper-shaped gold *cornicellos* to ward off the *malocchio*, the evil eye – Keith has a confession fetish, and he needs to get this off his chest. He'll have to go to a priest, too, sooner or later. But first his parents – tied in with God, as Keith perceives things – have to forgive him. He takes me aside and tells me all this – that he's going to come out with everything – one second after his mother unloads on me. A cigarette burns between his fingers as he stabs the air. That crazy wire hair, a red cowboy bandanna tying it off just above his eyebrows.

I'm already sorry I've showed up, but I promised Keith. I'm here, too, because I don't feel like being alone. My parents won't be home from their restaurant jobs until the first many hours of 1973 have exploded. My dad, right now, in his maroon vest and bowtie, double times it across the dining room of the Park Schenley with a tray of indescribably delicious, expensive entrees for a table of eight swells who've had too much to drink and don't give the slightest shit about him. But he knows this, and it doesn't faze him one iota. He doesn't care about them, either. He wants what's in their wallets, and he might even have to kiss their asses a little to get some of it. My mother won't kiss anyone's ass. Wearing a too-short dress and go-go boots, she's hostessing – refereeing, really – at The Suicide King, a strip joint a few blocks from the Park Schenley. Because she feels so cheated by life, so squandered, she'd burn down the building with every dirty, slavering bastard in it and not think twice about it.

I remind myself that this is a celebration. The Gentiles love their New Year's Eve, and they're trying to love it, even this year, with all the heartache Keith laid on their doorstep – and they don't even know the half of it. These people, including me, year after year, play poker, eat sauerkraut and kielbasa, drink beer and whiskey until midnight, when Mrs. Gentile hauls out an Italian feast. Like being with family – the benefits, the hazards. Crazy people, but I'm used to crazy people.

I take a seat at the kitchen table. It's me, Keith, Keith's dad, and Keith's younger brother, Nicholas – everyone calls him Gizzi – who's mentally retarded. Keith's mother plays, too. Before he dropped out, Keith had been a Special Ed major – because of Gizzi. He wanted to help kids like his brother.

Gizzi meticulously stacks his change, by denomination, in silver columns. He wears a black Franco Harris football jersey: number 32. Earlier in the day, the Steelers lost in the American Football Conference Championship Game, 21-17, to the undefeated Miami Dolphins, which ended a season filled with epiphany.

Everyone loves Franco and his Italian Army. Just the week before, against the son-of-a-bitch Oakland Raiders, with mere seconds left on the clock and the Steelers trailing, Franco made that unbelievable, pinball-machine, optical-illusion catch that some Catholic guy, Michael Ord, who had been at Three Rivers for the game, later christened, from atop a table in a downtown bar, the Immaculate Reception. This Ord guy said: "It was the synchronicity of universal events. It was destined to happen. It was going to happen. We just didn't know it was going to happen." A miracle – that launched the Steelers into the big

AFC showdown with the Dolphins. Franco, with his Afro and beard, his muscles, looked like Hercules when he was interviewed in the locker room after the game. I guess we're all a little blue about today's loss. Five lousy points away from the Super Bowl.

We always play the same game, five-card stud, all night – simple, clean, and requires no imagination, just balls – because of Gizzi, who's pretty hep, pretty regular, but intricacy plays havoc with him. Simplicity suits me fine. The last thing I want to do is think, and I'm coming out of my skin wondering when Keith – across the table from me, twitching, smoking, his eyebrows going up and down as if he's flashing me code – is going to drop the bomb about the abortion. He's about to explode himself.

Gizzi calls five-card stud *Nigger Poker.* He says it innocently enough. He means no harm. I've heard it called this plenty of times before, but it always bothers me. The first time he says it, Mrs. Gentile says, "That's not nice, Honey." Mr. Gentile ignores it. Keith just looks uncomfortable, like *What are you going to do?*

We ante. Mr. Gentile deals the first hand: first card down, the next four up. A little like my dad, he keeps everything to himself, a good guy in a plain white T-shirt, bald, round, and powerful. Mike Gentile, a union man. We play nickel, dime, quarter. Quarter is top bump – no exceptions. This is a friendly game.

On the table is a big pan of sauerkraut and kielbasa and a plate of Kaiser rolls from Rimini's Bakery. All the men, except Gizzi – who drinks pop, like Mrs. Gentile – have shots of Old Crow and Iron City ponies in front of them. Mrs. Gentile doesn't drink, and she doesn't like it that her husband allows Keith and me to drink underage.

"Mike," she says when Mr. Gentile pours the shots,

and she looks at him.

"It's okay, Theresa," he says.

She's got the king of spades showing, so she opens with a dime. Mr. Gentile whistles and says, "Whatta you got under there, Theresa?"

"Wouldn't you like to know?"

I've got a ten of hearts showing, with a seven underneath. Nothing much else around the table.

Everybody sees the bet, and Mr. Gentile deals. Gizzi, next to me on my left, with a four showing, catches an ace, so the bet's to him. He doesn't say a word, just carefully peels a quarter from his stack and flicks it, across the red oilcloth, stenciled with white poinsettias, into the pot.

"Honey, that's a big bet," Mrs. Gentile says. "Are you sure, Sweetheart?"

"Yes," Gizzi says.

Mr. Gentile whistles again, and everyone throws in a quarter.

Gizzi catches a four on the next round, giving him a pair of them, along with that ace. He flicks two quarters this time into the pot.

"Only one quarter, Honey," Mrs. Gentile says, and returns one of the quarters to Gizzi's stack. He looks like he doesn't like it. We all drop quarters into the pot.

The fifth and last card is dealt. I catch another ten for a pair. Mrs. Gentile catches her second nine for a pair. Keith and Mr. Gentile have nothing showing. Gizzi's showing those fours. I have the high hand on the table, so the bet's to me – and here it's tricky. Gizzi's not a bad player – he can mainly hold his own at a poker table – but I don't want to beat him. A pair of tens is a hell of hand in a five-card game, but who knows?

I glance at Gizzi. He's rocking back and forth, a habit when he plays, and gazing into my eyes. He's got blond hair and blond peach fuzz on his lip and chin, big black glasses over egg-blue eyes. He looks just like the Gentiles – chiseled features, the skeletal face – but he's fair, and the rest of them are dark. He's kind of smiling. I check the bet, trying to take it easy on him, do the right thing – though of course he might be sitting on something underneath that'll give him trips or two pair. It's to Gizzi. He scoots two quarters into the pot.

"No, Honey, remember. Just one quarter," says Mrs. Gentile and again places the second quarter on Gizzi's stack. He gives her that same look.

We go around the table. Keith folds. Mr. Gentile folds. Mrs. Gentile, with her pair of nines, folds. It's just me and Gizzi. What am I supposed to do? I got him beat on the table. I see his quarter and call. Gizzi turns his hole card over, a five, and smiles like he just kicked my ass. But all he has is that pair of fours.

"Good hand, Fritz," Mr. Gentile says to me. He pats Gizzi on the back. "You almost had him, Son. You ran the rest of us out of the game."

It's only then that Gizzi seems to get that he hasn't won. His smile disappears. He takes off his glasses, breathes on each lens, buffs them with his Franco jersey and puts them back on.

"I just got lucky, Giz," I say.

"Lucky," he repeats.

Mr. Gentile picks up his shot. Keith and I hoist ours. Mrs. Gentile holds her glass in the air.

"Get your drink, Gizzi," Mrs. Gentile says. "Do *Saluto* with us."

Gizzi raises his glass.

"Saluto," pronounces Mr. Gentile and bolts back the Old Crow. Keith and I drain ours, then chase them with beer. Gizzi says "Salute" and everyone laughs. He and Mrs. Gentile clink glasses across the table and drink.

It's my pot, but I don't want to touch it. Keith is contemplating something, all circuits firing in a jumble. His eyes look like a ventriloquist dummy's. You can hear them clicking. His hair fizzes. He's trying like hell to smile, but he's grimacing, a lit cigarette smoldering between bared teeth. He's about to out with it – the abortion – and what'll I do? I have my own confession to make.

Keith had planned to keep the baby – the baby the Gentiles think is still growing in Bonnie's womb – and marry Bonnie, put his shoulder to the wheel for the next sixty or seventy years and gut it out until the priest showed up to anoint him on his death bed. Bonnie, however, insisted on the abortion; she couldn't bring such *disgrazia* – a baby out of wedlock – home to her Old World parents. Bonnie and Keith didn't have enough money for the abortion, so I chipped in.

I watched Bonnie, like a martyr walking into Nero's torture chamber, disappear behind the downtown clinic's metal door. I waited with Keith and handed him cigarettes and told him there was nothing else they could have done when he termed what was going on, on the other side of the door, murder.

"Bullshit," I told him every time he declared he was now cursed forever, like someone had put the *malocchio* on him, that he and Bonnie had sinned, that he'd be called to answer. "It's okay, Man. There's nothing else you could've done." I said it because I wanted it to all be over, for Bonnie to trip back into the waiting room like nothing had ever happened. I said it because of my part in it. I was talking to myself. *Is it a sin? Does it carry a curse, some comeuppance, like a bullet with your name on it that'll someday plow through your brain because you fucked with the wrong person?* I don't know shit. That's what I know.

One Sunday night, when I was eight or nine years

old, I had burst into our house on Saint Marie Street, after playing outside. Walter Cronkite's Jehovah-like voice flooded the living room. Splashed across the screen of our big boxy black-and-white TV was *Abortion and the Law,* a CBS News Special Report. When I asked what *abortion* meant, my mother and father shot each other panicked looks, and I knew I should have never opened my mouth – the way they stared at each other, as if I'd spied them at something dirty. They never answered. I kissed them goodnight – I was still young enough to do that – then I climbed up to my room and crawled in bed, though it was well before my bedtime. They called after me: *Good night, sleep tight, don't let the bed bugs bite.* My dad had knocked up my mother with me in a West Virginia motel.

Bonnie returned to us, twitchy and drained, trying to smile, and reached for Keith's cigarette. Then we took her back to their apartment and put her to bed, looking herself like a baby, with the face of a forty-year-old.

I finally scrape up my pot.

"Your deal, Giz," Mr. Gentile says.

Gizzi gathers up the cards. He has all the moves: the overhand shuffle, then the riffle and cascade. He makes those cards mind, like they're drilling just for him – whisper and whoosh – that little bit of breeze chuffing out of them. "Ante," he says, and everyone throws in a nickel. Then he says, "Nigger Poker," smiles, and expertly whips the cards around the table.

"Nicholas," Mrs. Gentile says to him, maybe the tiniest break in her voice. "That's really not nice. You shouldn't say that." She looks at Mr. Gentile, like it's his fault, but he ignores her and pours another round.

This time Gizzi wins, and everyone is relieved. We eat big sloppy sandwiches of sauerkraut and kielbasa, pickles, hot Polish mustard that Mr. Gentile brought home from one of his mill-hunk buddies at Mesta, drink beer and whiskey, and light one cigarette after another. The kitchen mantles in smoke.

I mainly play blind, rarely looking at my hole card, seeing most bets, folding whenever I can. Nobody notices. I win two more hands – because it's impossible not to: trip deuces up on my first three cards and then a pair of mustached kings up on another. The rest of them I let go, even if I have the table outgunned with my hole card. I don't want to take a chance on beating Gizzi. Maybe the rest of them are doing the same thing.

Gizzi wins most hands, stacks his winnings into pillars, throttles the deck like a sharp when the deal comes back to him and, each time, announces *Nigger Poker* and smiles. Mrs. Gentile stops correcting him, but looks at Big Mike menacingly. He doesn't say a word, yanks a pocket knife from his trousers, and digs at his fingernails. He eats and he pours and, every once in a while, he grabs our empty ponies, pitches them under the sink, and plops fresh bottles from the fridge in front of us.

Mrs. Gentile leaves for a moment and turns on the TV in the living room. Guy Lombardo broadcasts from the Waldorf Astoria. It's 11:30. The sauce revs on the stovetop. It's almost time to put the water on for Mrs. Gentile's homemade ravioli. Soon we'll watch the big glittering ball crash into Times Square and parrot the countdown – *5, 4, 3, 2, 1* – hold hands, kiss *Buon Anno,* sing "Auld Lang Syne," then eat macaroni and drink Dago Red.

It might be that the Gentiles are coming around to the idea of the baby. I can hear them: *It's not the baby's fault that Bonnie and Keith have made the biggest mistakes of their lives. Why should the baby suffer?* The Gentiles are Italian people; they adore children. They'll doubly love this baby. They'll start putting money away for its education. Nobody's going to take it out on the baby. And, besides, Keith is their only chance at grandchildren. Gizzi's never going to get married.

Keith is about to devour his cards. Like a prelude to something utterly fantastic, he emanates a vibrato thrum, a soundtrack of building dread. He moves preternaturally, robotically. He hears something, something inside of him – that I begin to hear, too. Like a heartbeat. Like the madman narrator in "A Tell-Tale Heart." Keith throws me an imploring gaze as if warning me that he's about to blow. He glances around the table, at his mother and father, Gizzi, back to me. *No,* I insist telepathically.

Gizzi's got the deal again and, when he announces *Nigger Poker,* Keith stands abruptly and knocks against the table. Bottles and glasses quake. Gizzi's columns of change wobble. We all turn to Keith. *Okay,* I think. *Here goes.*

Keith collects himself, straightens and, with a pained look, braces himself on the table. "Don't say that anymore, Giz. Okay?" he says shakily.

Gizzi's temple of change collapses. He stares in disbelief at the heap of silver, then begins to cry. The clock is an inch from midnight.

The Gazebo

(for Suzanne)

To escape the summer heat of Claire's apartment, she and I drove to David's, the theatre on Walnut Street in Shadyside, to see *Citizen Kane.* One of Claire's professors at Pitt had screened it in class, and she was convinced that I should see it. I was glad to go, mainly for the air conditioning, but I would have done anything to please her. After the movie, we walked a few paces to the Gazebo, a delicatessen Claire was enchanted with.

As I listened to Claire talk about the movie – she called it "brilliant," "a miracle" – and maybe it was – I knew I hadn't been paying attention. She said Kane is a guy who tries to fill up his emptiness with things, attempting to buy heart and soul with money and power; an indictment of Capitalism; a living, breathing Marxist allegory. I didn't disagree, though I didn't know anything about Marx, but Kane is not unlike the rest of us. He just seems much more fortunate than most. After all, even though he has issued from down-on-their-luck working stiffs, he ends up with money and power and, for a while, he is young and handsome and, who knows, maybe even fleetingly happy – way more than most of us can expect.

The people I came from – a different batch of

down-on-their-luck working stiffs – did not have money or power and had little prospects for either. Their emptiness gnawed holes in them. I don't remember much about what I contributed to this conversation about *Citizen Kane*. I might have just sat there and listened and not said a word. Kane has a heart. I liked him, I liked the movie, and you don't have to be in college, which I wasn't, to get "Rosebud."

That late afternoon in the Gazebo with Claire, I wanted clarity – not parables. More than anything, I was reminded of something I knew to be absolutely *ex cathedra* true but had never really allowed myself to dwell on: everything means something else. Not only that, but everybody is also somebody else. It's hard to make your way when things aren't what they seem, and I suppose Charles Foster Kane knows that all along. Surely Orson Welles, the man who made the film, in 1941, when he was only twenty-five, just five years older than I was that very warm day, keenly understood this.

Claire was not beautiful; some would say not even pretty. She had recently cut her long, brown hair. It barely covered her ears, bangs chopped to an inch of her scalp line. Eyebrows heavy and arched, thin nose with the slightest hook to it. Enormous silvery eyes; bowed, exaggerated lips. Immaculate skin – like a baby's. She looked like Our Lady of Guadalupe, and I was pleased to be with her. I was fascinated by her willingness to say what she felt. Before my romance with Claire, I had never set foot inside the Gazebo. I had known it existed, but it wasn't a place I would have ever entered on my own. Perhaps, I was a little intimidated by what I perceived as its high tone. But, then again, I would have never gone to see *Citizen Kane* of my own volition, either.

An older woman in a royal blue sleeveless dress

sprinkled with giant sunflowers walked over to our table. She wore three or four bracelets on either wrist. Her hair was dyed bright orange, her heavily wrinkled face caked with make-up. She stood there for an awkward amount of time and stared at me. I was about to say something when she said, "You don't know who I am. Do you?"

I smiled. "I guess not."

"I'm Madeleine DeSantis. An old friend of your family."

I studied her. I had no idea who she was. As far as I knew, my family had no old friends.

She smiled, a big, orange lipsticked smile. Wrinkles branched across her face like an oracle. "Joseph David DelGreco," she whispered. "Little Joey. Joey DelGreco."

I looked into her tiny brown eyes.

"Little Joey," she whispered. "Look at you. You're a grown man."

I sat there and smiled.

"You remember me, don't you?" Madeleine asked. She took my face in her hands. "You couldn't forget old Madeleine."

"Of course, I remember you, Madeleine," I said. "It just took me a minute. How could I ever forget you? How have you been?"

Still with my face vised between her hands, Madeleine gazed at me soulfully, held me like that for a long moment, our eyes locked, tears in hers, then gave me a big kiss on the lips. From across the table, I felt Claire's incredulity.

I stood and pulled out a chair. "Please, Madeleine, sit with us."

"For one minute," she said. "I have a table toward the back."

I held the chair for her, slipped it under her as she

sat and, as I did, she reached back and patted my hand. I sat and motioned to Claire. "Madeleine, this is Claire Raffo."

"I'm so charmed," Madeleine said, lurching up from her chair and across the table. Claire, in a similar move, met her mid-table, where they bridged, then kissed and held each other.

"It's wonderful to meet you, Madeleine," she said. "I've heard so much about you." Claire was now complicit, all in like me, playing along.

What the heck, I thought. "Claire and I are engaged." I chanced a quick glance at Claire. She looked at me and smiled.

"Oh, my God!" Madeleine exclaimed, then kissed me, made the bridge with Claire again, and kissed me another time when she sat down. "That is just the most wonderful news. But so young. You're so young. But listen to me. It's none of my business. When you find the right one – and I know this because I was seventeen when I married my Prince Charming – you know." She wagged a finger. "You two know exactly what I'm talking about. Don't you?"

Claire and I beamed. I even felt it – as if we were really getting married. I reached across the table, and Claire took my hand.

"When's the big day?" Madeleine asked.

"We're in no rush," Claire said. "Maybe a year or so."

"You're smart," said Madeleine. "I'm so nosy, but I have to see the ring."

Claire removed her left hand from her lap and slid it across the table to Madeleine: a slender silver band with a fake jade pebble at its crown. I had been with Claire when she bought it for a dollar at the Red Quill, a five and ten across the street.

"Oh, my God!" said Madeleine, this time in a near shriek that occasioned glances toward our table. "That's just gorgeous! I'm so happy for you two. God love you both. Such exciting news." Then to me: "I know how happy your grandmother is about this."

"She's ecstatic," I said without hesitation.

"How is she?" Madeleine asked. "It's been forever, I don't know how long, since she and I talked. She told me you're at Bucknell, and you're going to be a lawyer like your papa. She's so proud. She didn't mention the wedding."

"Joey proposed just a week ago," said Claire, covering like a champ.

I instantly liked being Joey DelGreco and had the knack for it, too. I wore a white shirt, jeans, and flip-flops. I was thin and strong and tan from working construction all summer. I had just seen *Citizen Kane* with my mysterious fiancé with whom I sipped coffee and ate Reuben sandwiches, latkes, and apple sauce. I was bright and handsome: I studied pre-law at Bucknell. I was Joseph David DelGreco. Little Joey – which might mean my dad was Big Joey DelGreco, a gunslinger lawyer, maybe a kingpin racketeer, who'd long ago salted away my ample inheritance.

But there was the matter of this grandmother of mine whom Madeleine had mentioned. And what the hell, really, was I doing – and Claire too – perpetuating this masquerade? My mother's name – my real mother – was Rita Sweeney, Rita Schiaretta Sweeney. My dad – my real dad – was Travis Sweeney, whose parents had died before my birth. My real mother's real mother, my only grandmother, whom I had rarely seen, was also dead. She and my mother had shared an unspeakable secret that had something to do with my mother's father, Federico, after whom I was named, who perished when his cobbler shop had inexplicably burned to the ground in 1942. Rita's life – and, by extension my history, my very birthright – was a vast, labyrinthine estate, like Kane's Xanadu, a maze of triple-locked rooms to which I was forbidden entry.

But Joey DelGreco's grandmother was fine, absolutely thriving. I had just seen her Sunday, three days ago, when the whole family, as usual, dropped in on her. This is what I told Madeleine.

"Marvelous," she said. "I bet she made pizza."

"Nobody makes pizza like my grandma."

"And that divine chocolate cake with seafoam icing. A masterpiece."

I smiled and nodded.

"You look just like your grandfather, Giuseppe, a good man. You were named for him. Gone too young." Tears again appeared in her eyes.

I smiled and nodded again, then slightly bowed my head out of respect for my new dead grandfather.

"You're a good boy," Madeleine said, as if to reward me. Then to Claire: "How about you, Honey? Are you in school?"

"I'm at Pitt, studying Psychology."

"God love you young people," she said. "So smart. Minds of your own. Nobody tells you what to do." Then back to me, darting in to kiss me again. "I can't get over how handsome and grown up." She motioned toward me and said to Claire: "Since diapers, I've known this one. Now look at him. Look at you both. Like movie stars. Important people."

"What about you, Madeleine? How are you?" Claire asked.

Madeleine slightly lifted her hand from the table, fingers splayed in a spider, a gesture so familiar, so exquisite – that meant, in essence, *What does it matter?*

"I do fine," she said. "I stay busy. I need to be in closer touch with people like Joey's grandmother."

Claire took her hand from mine, reached across the table and patted Madeleine's hand. "Come sit with us, Madeleine. There's plenty of room. Join us, please?"

"I don't want to intrude on you young people. I just had to say hello. I couldn't believe my eyes when I saw Little Joey sitting here. I shouldn't call him *Little.*"

"You can call him anything you'd like, Madeleine," Claire said.

"That's absolutely true, Madeleine," I added. "We'd love for you to sit with us."

"You're nice," she said. "I'd love to. I'll be right back. All I have is coffee."

Madeleine nipped off, and Claire and I looked at each other.

"What in hell are you doing, Joey?" she asked.

"I don't know. But you're doing it, too. Why'd you ask her to sit with us? How will we get out of this?"

"She's lonesome."

"I know."

"I love you," Claire said.

Claire had never said that to me before. I don't think anyone had said that to me before. She had fallen for Joey DelGreco.

It was obvious Madeleine had me mixed up with someone else, and, instead of stringing her along, I should have told her from the outset that I wasn't Joey DelGreco. I was Fritz Sweeney (Claire called me, exclusively, *Frederick,* my given name, and had once told me that "No one is just a Fritz"). But I didn't want to part with this new persona that had been handed me by a stranger who seemed to know me from elsewhere. A better me, the me I aspired to. Madeleine – whom I liked very much, and she clearly liked me – was suddenly part of my life, or this other life of mine, as Joey DelGreco, that I had my foot in the door of and tried to imagine. Kane forgets who he is and exchanges one life for another – a kind of amnesia that surely afflicts many from time to time.

And, of course, I was having a good time, being clever and feeling important, deftly improvising an entire identity at the expense of Madeleine. Sooner or later, I'd hit a dead end, and Madeline would find me out. But I wanted to go on with the charade a little longer and see where it led. For the moment, I didn't want to go back to being Fritz Sweeney. Claire could have halted it instantly as well, yet she had signed on without hesitation.

A future with Claire would be a maze from which I'd never emerge: navigating a life of interminable interpretation, nothing black and white, neither yes nor no, nothing settled, dead end after dead end. Claire seemed able to see into that future, but I could not. I knew she and I would never marry, or maybe I knew we should never marry. Nevertheless, as Joey DelGreco, with whom Claire was so smitten, I was prepared that night to spirit her and that dollar ring off to the all-night Ordinary and disastrously declare, "Till death do us part."

Madeleine rejoined us with her little cup of coffee and dainty saucer. I stood until she sat.

"Such a gentleman," she said. "Such gorgeous manners. That's what comes from the right upbringing. Our people, when they came over here, had not a cent to their names, couldn't even speak the language, treated like scum. Then the Depression. Then the war. Me and your grandmother. We could tell stories. But now, look at you and this beautiful girl. Seeing you two, all the hardship and sacrifice was worth it."

It looked like Madeleine might break down, but she took a sip of coffee, and smiled. "Listen to me, boring you two college people. Don't let your food get cold. *Mangiare.* You know what that means?"

When we nodded, she laughed uproariously.

Madeleine's hand shook as she brought the cup to her lips. Her eyes were wet.

"Are you alright, Madeleine?" Claire asked.

"Oh, I'm fine, Honey. You know . . . the old gray mare. I'll be 81 in April. It just creeps up on you and has no mercy."

"You look terrific," Claire said. "I hope I look half as good when I'm your age. But have you eaten? Have you had supper?"

"Look at me. Do I look like I'm on a diet? I eat all the time. Maybe just a little more coffee."

"Maybe you need a little something to eat."

"Claire's right, Madeleine. A little food will perk you up."

"I should be treating you two kids, but after all these years, now on a fixed income, I still have to watch my pennies. But who's complaining? Every once in a while, I come in here. Reminds me of the good old days. My husband, Benny, and I came here all the time. We'd listen to jazz at the Gaslight, have a few cocktails, then stroll arm in arm across the street for corned beef sandwiches in this very room. He's gone nineteen years. March 29."

The tears stalled in her eyes rolled down her cheeks, just the two, in unison. She dabbed at them with her napkin. I patted her shoulder. Claire hadn't touched her food. She placed half her Reuben and two latkes on an empty saucer and stationed it in front of Madeleine. "Share this with me," she said.

"Oh, Honey, my God, I can't accept this."

"I'll never eat all of it," Claire assured her.

"God love you two."

Madeleine seemed more animated, more with it suddenly. Maybe it was the food which she ate with relish. When the waiter strolled by, we ordered cheesecake and more coffee.

It was after five o'clock. Folks filtered in for beer and sandwiches. Young people with real jobs in dresses, khaki, and seersucker suits; aging old-money Pittsburgh, Madeleine's age, in denim and madras wraparounds and summer jumpers, Lacoste shirts with that infantile alligator on the left breast, sockless in penny and tassel loafers.

The bar instantly packed. Waiters and waitresses peeled out the swinging kitchen doors with trays of food. My real parents, Travis and Rita Sweeney, worked in restaurants, at least my dad did. My mother was a hostess at an almost unmentionable joint on Baum Boulevard. The sun, streaking the tables, leaned on the immense window front of The Gazebo. A beam singled out Madeleine and, for a moment, she was thirty years younger. With great pomp, she rose from the table.

"Running into you two this afternoon has been such a gift – to see you, Joey, after all these years, and your beautiful bride-to-be. And thank you for sharing your food and the cheesecake and all of it. Believe me when I say I can't remember the last time I enjoyed myself like this."

"Why don't you stay another few minutes?" Claire said.

"I'm going to walk down to the corner and catch the 73 back to East Liberty. I still live in our little place on Lenora Street. It's getting bad down there, but where am I going to go? Home is home – the house Benny and I moved into when we first married. We never had children, twice almost . . . I'm just thankful to have a roof over my head."

Claire and I stood. We embraced Madeleine and kissed her. She dipped into her purse and produced a small heart-shaped casket with a mother-of-pearl patina, a gold cross at its center. She placed it in Claire's hand.

"Open it," she said.

Inside was a delicate silver rosary with tiny crystal beads. Christ's nimbus fanned the transverse beams of the crucifix; at His feet furled *Italia.*

Claire sat back down and covered her mouth with her hands. "Madeleine," she whispered, then she cried softly through her hand. "It's too beautiful."

"This is just a little something, an early wedding present. Whatever you want to call it. Congratulations, and God Bless you."

"We can't accept this, Madeleine," I said.

"It's nothing. Honest to God. What am I going to do with this kind of stuff? My house is filled with it, like that – what's it called – the Sacred Heart of Jesus Store down on Liberty Avenue. And give your grandmother, your whole family, my love. Tell them old Madeline said hello. Madeleine DeSantis. And tell them shame on me for not being in better touch."

"I'll do that, Madeline," I said.

She patted my cheek, and said, "Don't forget me. I've never forgotten you."

Then she walked out the door and disappeared into the summer evening thrall that awaited Claire and me.

⁂

The Act of Contrition

Praying the sky would open with diluvial vengeance, washing away my daily trial with brick and mortar, I hunkered with the others, smoking bummed cigarettes under the unshingled, leaking eaves of one of the two dozen houses we were bricking way out in Rowena Township. We waited for that last sputtering candle of green sun to snuff in the thunderheads, so we could head for early morning shots and beers at the bar, then home for a day we were helpless to retrieve: eight hours of pay twirling down the sump with the floodwaters.

The guys prayed like me, though not so fervently, that my Uncle Pat, who owned and ruled the outfit, would throw his head in the direction he threw it when he was dismissing something as bullshit or out of his omniscient control. Forbidding as a crazed Catholic idol, meditating on how best to son-of-a-bitch the world he seemed to hold in the palm of his hand, Pat sat inscrutably behind the wheel of his red pick-up. The electricians, jobbed out to wire the new houses, had already split. The carpenters had stowed their tools, but had to stick it out with the rest of us, shivering, drenched, pissed off, cussing Pat, waiting for him to make the call.

A locomotive of thunder exploded above our heads. The temperature had fallen twenty degrees.

Lightning swung up from the distant river – its electrical scent in the rain – and arced in a splayed fretwork of fangs over the blackening site. Up in the swirling firmament, a new yowling constellation of spiders and octopi, every jagged creature, revealed itself.

Pat started his truck and drove slowly by. He jabbed his head at us, a rueful smile, though no smile at all, that meant we were free to go: go to hell. Whatever. The guys stepped out into the storm, headed for the bar, a string of hootches and a dry place to smoke. Pat braked the truck and beckoned me, not quite a nod. A barely noticeable flinch. Maybe an eyebrow. But I knew it was me he wanted. He never said my name. I was a pronoun, sometimes a *he* or a *him,* but often an *it,* more a *that.* I hadn't been on the job long enough to collect wages, so I wondered what might appear after *Pay to the Order of* on my first paycheck.

In fact, I hadn't heard my name fall out of Pat's mouth since I'd known him. And I had known him all my life, though I'd seen almost nothing of him except for holidays – that is, if those movable feasts fell on a day in the liturgical calendar when he and my mother happened to be speaking or inclined to occupy the same room together.

Pat was my mother's older brother, and there was bad blood between them. Something had happened, when I'm not sure, but it went unnamed, snubbed for so long that they had forgotten what exactly had initially triggered the breach – though every bit of poison that coursed their veins stemmed from the fiery death of their father, Federico, when his cobbler shop torched. The grand efficiency of vendetta, however – an engine of such agonized festering – is that, over time, it no longer requires reason or narrative. It is a force, an element, every bit as impervious as the mighty rain that sent the entire crew, except me, home for the day.

Whatever it was between my mother and Pat was buried in a shallow grave, a cenotaph in an overgrown forgotten cemetery. They nurtured their grudge like lovers nurture love; and, of course, it was, had all along been, love – of whatever lethal ilk – between my Uncle Patrick Schiaretta and my mother, Rita Schiaretta, who had become Rita Sweeney when she married my father, the Irishman, Travis Sweeney. My father figured powerfully into the story, though how remained another mystery. Different than all other men I found myself around, the perfect father for me, he refused to mix in melodrama of any kind. He didn't willingly contribute his spleen to anything, though he loved every pathological cell in my mother's body – but would never fight Pat, or anyone else, for her. His courage was the fact that he was unapologetically himself every minute of his life. Where I grew up, however, in East Liberty, that amounted to no courage whatsoever, and he was punished – more by my mother than anyone – all of his life for not being another kind of man entirely, the kind of man she hated, and loved, like Pat, her executioner.

Had Pat spit my name, *Fritz*, out his truck window, it would have been a concession to my mother, even an admission. She knew how that game worked and played it flawlessly, with Spartan dedication. Nevertheless, she was hurt by her feud with Pat. She had a heart; he was born without one.

And there was Shotty Montesanto, who took pity on me, gave me his spare gloves and work boots and a lift to and from the job. He and Pat had come up friends, way way back on Omega Street, where my mother and her brothers had grown up. Shotty blamed Pat for the accident that had left Shotty crippled. One of my uncle's rigged-out shitty scaffolds had collapsed with Shotty troweling the last brick into a four-storey gable and left him with a bad limp. He laid brick every day for my uncle – like an artisan from ancient Rome, the acknowledged virtuoso mason of Pat's crew – but he wouldn't go near scaffold. Shotty worked exclusively with both feet on earth, and Pat never crossed him on this. Thus, Pat and Shotty had a mortal wound between them, as well, yet Shotty, too, still loved my uncle.

Shotty knew my parents, from way back, when they were all growing up. Shotty knew, too, I'm certain, what was up between my mother and Pat, but he'd never say; and he, like me, thrived on an imagined rendition of life – one that kept us from jumping from a bridge, like a number of the neighborhood desperate, especially the junkies, in the waning years of Vietnam.

I had signed on with Pat as a hod carrier, and it had gone disastrously. The hod, whether filled with brick or mortar, was simply too heavy, too unwieldy, for me to manage. So, I carried mortar in five-gallon buckets and toted bricks in brick tongs and became the *straccione* laughing stock of the crew. Gutting out the summer with Pat was something I'd have to bear – the equivalent of honor where I came from. I dreamed of quitting from the first moment I punched in. My father saw quitting Pat as mere inevitability, good judgment, even, whereas my mother viewed it as epic betrayal – of her. My carrying a hod for Pat was a way of vindicating her. She needed me to fill the hole in her; my dad couldn't do it. He didn't possess the script. More than anything, he didn't possess the Italian blood. Days on the job were excruciatingly long: blazing sun and filth, muscles that whimpered every time I lifted in each blistered hand a bucket of mud and tottered toward the mortarboards, the impatient bricklayers belittling my every mincing step.

I was already facing disgrace the day my uncle summoned me in the deluge over to his truck. I stood at the driver's window, which he had rolled down. Water cascaded off me. Lightning and thunder corrugated the cobalt sky. The rain blew in on him. His face was the color of brick, the chiseled bust of Lucifer – nimbused with electricity, terrifyingly handsome – before tumbling into his lake of fire. His teeth glinted – it was plenty cold by then – and his breath as he spoke smoked out of his mouth: "See that house with the light. You're going over there to work with Kenny."

Then he pulled off, zigging in the muddy red scurf wending out of the site. There were a few houses in the development we were bricking where families had already begun moving in, though not yet living in them. They had baby trees in the yards, trunks taped like the fetlocks of quarter horses, guy wires bracing them so they'd grow straight. Straw spread the lawns, and empty, giant appliance cartons, collapsed in the rain, sat in the road at the bottom of their driveways. I slogged toward the house with a single bulb glowering in its ornate fixture over a basement door.

The other guys, invisible behind their slapping windshield wipers, followed in a cortege behind Pat. The last was Shotty in his gold Bonneville. He rolled down his window. "Where you going, *manovale?* You walking home? Get in the car."

"Pat told me I gotta go up there and work with Kenny." I nodded toward the house.

"How the hell you gonna get home?"

"I don't know."

He cranked up his window three-quarters – he was getting soaked – so that all I saw were his eyes and widow's peak. "Listen. Watch out for that fat bastard. One sick mother-huncher. Quasi-fuckin-modo." He tapped his temple. *"Puzza."* Then he sealed the window, shot me a bemused scary look, wavy beneath the curtain of water sweeping over the glass, and slid out of sight toward Sunset's Tavern in Aspinwall and a breakfast that would start with a shot of Imperial chased by a shimmering green Rolling Rock pony.

I was drenched to the skin by the time I got to the back door of that house. Sidled up to it was a banged-up mortar mixer chained to one of the columns supporting a little thatched roof. Next to the mixer sat a fifty-five-gallon drum of water. And two immense pallets – of firebrick and antique brick. Out in the sparse new grass of the backyard was a swing set with a yellow plastic slide.

I walked through the door – I nearly knocked – and there sat Kenny Fortuna on a stack of full mortar bags, smoking a cigarette, drinking buttermilk; his busted-up fingers thick as knockwurst; a nasty Pittsburgh Pirates cap cocked back on his head; heavy black glasses, taped at the hinges; four or five days of white stubble spackling his weathered face. Coated with mortar and construction filth – like leftover aggregate coughed out of the rotating giant bowels of the cement mixer – you'd need a brick hammer to hack him out of the crusty, caked green work clothes he never changed. Bitterness pooled in his eyes, cold and gray, pupils like the jagged heads of finishing nails. Behind him was a mammoth unfinished fireplace, a clean mortar board, and a red Folgers coffee tin of water to temper the mortar.

Kenny had hated me at first glimpse, my inaugural morning on the job, when I had proved so hopeless at the hod. He'd been laying block, fetching up those thirty-pound slabs with one hand, like they were shoeboxes, and troweling them one atop another in a perfect plumb line into the foundation he was building. Shotty referred to Kenny as *cockstrong* – a Herculean might that emanated from some long-nurtured injury or insult; a fulminating diabolic fury, kept barely in check. That first morning he laid eyes on me, Kenny had turned toward me and grabbed a quart carton of Meadow Gold buttermilk, suffering on his puffed flinty lips a kind of smile, as I staggered again and again beneath the weight of the impossible hod.

"Forget about him," Shotty had advised about Kenny." He's an *animale,* a sour sloppy piece of *merda.* He wipes his fat Calabrese ass with a mortar sack. Somebody should shoot him."

I kind of nodded at Kenny when I entered the cellar. He didn't flinch, just moved his bored gaze toward me, like a lazing sated lion, but said nothing, for maybe a minute, then flicked the cigarette, smoked down to a quarter-inch nub, in my direction. "Whatta you say, Matilda?"

Kenny, too, had a thing for Pat. In his rendition, he had been like a big brother to Pat, took him under his wing when Pat returned from the war puny, penniless, and all fucked up. Taught Pat everything he knew and fronted him the bread for his first truck and the worn-out bucks and scaffold Pat still used. They had been partners in the brick business that had made Pat a millionaire. The business Kenny had masterminded and Pat had jewed him out of. Like Pat had not merely swindled him, but jilted him, broken his heart, and that's what had turned him *cockstrong,* into a beast.

Shotty, who had been with Pat since that first truck over a quarter century ago, said Kenny's account was bullshit, and so did my mother when I asked her about it. She, my dad, and I had been sitting in the kitchen. Cigarette smoke streamed through the late afternoon sun stealing through the window. My dad was dressed for work from the waist down, but no shirt, and he hadn't shaved yet. In a black half-slip and black bra, my mother teased spongy, frizz-clotted curlers out of her bleached hair and dropped them on the kitchen table.

"He's a liar, Kenny Fortuna," my mother said. "Don't believe a single thing that comes out of his filthy mouth. And he's ugly as sin and twice as stupid. He's a monster. I hate him." Then she lit a cigarette, as if that were my dad's cue to comment.

My father had worked with Kenny the few times he had labored for Pat. None of it had worked out well. But my father habitually refused comment other than the usual: *The truth doesn't matter. It never mattered. There is no truth.* And my mother would tell him that he was full of shit – though she knew, and I knew too, that my dad was right. Who knows what really happened? And, ultimately, it doesn't matter. People get something in their heads – right or wrong – and there it is. Forever.

"There's no need to hate him, Fritz," said my dad. "But he's worth keeping an eye on."

"I need to hate him," said my mother.

"He's unhappy. His wife's an invalid. Let's just be glad we're not him."

"His wife's a tramp," responded my mother. "Jesus Christ, Travis, when did you get so chummy with Kenny Fortuna? You always said he was the worst son of a bitch."

"I did say that, Rita, and I stand by that assessment, but nobody's just one thing."

"Shotty says he's shell-shocked from the war," I volunteered.

"He was never in the war." She looked at my dad.

"I think he was in the war, Rita."

"He was not in the goddam war."

My parents smoked cigarettes, and the three of us looked out the screen door where robins pompously strutted through our backyard grass that badly needed cutting. The dandelions' little white Afros tossed in the evening breeze. Kids played Wiffle Ball in the alley.

"I'd like to stick a knife in him," said my mother.

"For the love of God, Rita," said my dad.

"Exactly," she said, staring at the robins. Her lips twisted. She was murdering Kenny. But she might've been thinking about Pat.

"The rich," Kenny offered, as he lifted up off the mortar sacks. "One minute they want this; the next minute they want that. Their shithouses are fancier than the front room." The cellar had a full bathroom, bar and fridge and stove, a big color TV and couch, a little kids' blackboard, and balls and other toys strewn about. There were pictures on the walls. A pool table, the balls already racked, waiting to be busted apart; and a dozen cues, bracketed vertically in a glass cabinet. Like a magazine ad. "What the fuck are you looking at, Matilda? Mix me some mud. And start bringing that firebrick in."

I hoisted one of the seventy-pound bags he'd been perched on and staggered a few steps before getting it to my shoulder. Kenny watched in satisfaction. "Chip off the old block," he grunted. "This is a black mortar job, Matilda. You gotta mix in that shit by the door."

Next to the door were three two-pound bags of Solomon. I walked outside and busted open the sack on my shoulder into the mixer. Then went back in, grabbed one of the Solomons, and read the directions. I had never mixed up a batch of black mortar. You had to add just so much of the black Solomon to the aggregate before adding water. But the proportions were calibrated in kilograms: *2-10 kilograms for every 100 kilograms.* I shook out a couple of inches of black powder, mixed together the dry aggregates with a spade, dipped a five-gallon bucket in the barrel, threw in the water, and pulled the rip cord to start the mixer. It burbled and churned and sputtered up a black wave of filth across my face and chest before it stalled. I throttled it again, and it caught, beginning its methodical deafening grind, the mixer blades sluicing the aggregate and water together into grainy charcoal batter. I let it mix while I loaded brick tongs with firebrick, took them inside, and stacked them next to Kenny.

When I dumped the first pile of mixed mortar on Kenny's board, he yelled, "Jesus Christ, Matilda. You call this black? I want it black as the roots of your old lady's hair. Get it out of here."

So, Kenny was going to fuck with me the whole time. Call me *Matilda.* Insults all day. A little test: see how I'd roll with it, how much I could stand. I scraped the mortar from the board back into the bucket with a brick, then walked out, poured half the bag of Solomon in the mixer, a little more water, and revved it again.

"You're wearing more of that than you have in the bucket, Matilda," Kenny said when I appeared again. My shirt and hands were already black as grease. He began laying in the gorgeous fire brick, troweling their smooth alabaster faces with black mortar, slicing them in just so, perfect in every detail.

The entire morning, I hobbled outside, stood in the rain, spaded black mortar into the bucket, then manhandled it in and slopped it onto Kenny's mortar board, splashing him each time. His face flecked black. His glasses spotted. Black mortar coagulated in his whiskers. He smelled like a slaughterhouse. It pleased him that I was so inept. He stopped each time to watch me unload the mortar, never dodging the filth that ricocheted up in his face, laughing a deep, rumbling terrible laugh that cracked into convulsive hacks that subsided as he dragged on his Lucky, gulped the buttermilk, and croaked at intervals, "More mud, Matilda." Or: "More brick, Matilda."

I loitered outside on the little porch between trips in to Kenny – away from him and to catch a little blow. The rain came steady, slanting west, then east, as the wind shifted. Cold as hell. My bones chipped against one another. The road slicing from the site was a rusty orange swamp. Much further off, the Allegheny River stretched interminably, wide and green and cruel.

By lunch, I was done in, every inch of me a viscous heavy black that would never come out. I crouched against a block wall and ate my soggy sandwiches. Kenny, a black mess too, sat on the dwindling sacks of mortar, devoured his lunch in a few bites, and sipped buttermilk.

"Hey, Matilda. We look like a couple of *tizzones.*" He lumbered up toward me, his big plaster face jouncing, a cigarette smoldering in his lips. "Your old lady had a thing for me. Probably still does." Then he unzipped and took a piss right there on the cellar floor – a yard from where I was eating – returned to the enormous fireplace, crawled into it, like a bear in its den, drained what was left of the buttermilk, and began to snore.

I knew not to get sucked in by *Matilda* and those cracks about my mother and father. Kenny was an *animale.* I knew plenty of sour, vicious bastards like him in East Liberty. "Ignore him," my father would say. "He's not worth it." But my mother: she'd tell me to stick a knife in him. I knew what I was supposed to do: jump up and break his jaw. But my fist would've bounced off him like pea gravel off a brick wall, and then he would've beaten the living shit out of me.

How he loved that I was worthless as a laborer – like my dad had been worthless as a laborer. That fact made him feel very good about something. Vindicated. As if he was so much more broken-hearted than everyone else, his wound some epic secret no one could ever imagine or understand; yet, deep down, he wasn't bad at all, just in pain. But he'd never confess what the fuck it was. Rather, he'd take pleasure defaming the very oxygen he breathed, insisting everyone suffer right along with him: an East Liberty parable. Like those Buddhist priests I'd seen on TV douse themselves with gasoline, light a match, and just sit there in the Lotus, quaking in flame until they toppled over. My mother was one of those priests – and Pat, too. Kenny. Maybe even Shotty. They set themselves on fire, and everyone had to watch.

I thought about how best not to hate Kenny. Whatever had gone on with him and Pat was none of my affair. The hell with Pat. And whatever had gone on between Kenny and my parents: I didn't like that or what he said about them. But I didn't want to hate Kenny like my mother hated him – even if she had good reason – or how she hated other people. Shouldering vendetta is twice the weight of a hod. It ends up breaking you. Makes you cry out for mercy. I didn't need the grief – that hereditary machinery grinding away at me, my soul filled with concrete. I preferred my dad's resigned bemused detachment: as if he had gauged the underbelly of human nature so flawlessly, that to despise people for being assholes was like despising a bee for having a stinger. My dad simply did not believe in self-immolation.

Kenny's snoring, however, revolted me in ways I can't explain. It made me loathe him. It made me want to kill him. Literally. To make this feeling pass, since it shocked and terrified me – the sudden unfathomable homicidal anger I felt at everything that had anything to do with my life – I walked over to his slumped body, vibrating and bubbling like a cauldron, grabbed his cigarettes and lighter, lying next to him, and walked up the stairs into the house.

It smelled of Brand New – every inch of it gleamed – the aroma of fresh paint and newly nailed lumber and carpet never trod upon. Not a mark upon the yellow walls of the kitchen, the paler yellow humming refrigerator and range, dishwasher, the toaster and blender in green quilted sleeves festooned with tiny plastic strawberries. The stainless steel twin sinks and chrome fixtures. Cups dangling from tiny hooks beneath the cabinets. A kind of perfection that almost scared me. Even as I craved that very perfection, I preferred the mayhem of my home: my parents who worked nights at restaurants, who sat around half-clothed smoking cigarettes and drinking coffee and VO, and just letting things play out day by day. Not like this kitchen: all this unearthly planning, this insistence on but one version of truth – how to live a life and what a life is worth.

I almost started to hate the people who would eventually live there, whoever they might have been – I guess, maybe, because I wanted what they had. There was nothing wrong with wanting things. Then I wondered what my parents wanted. Did they want more than what they had? Did they have what they wanted? Surely not. It suddenly struck me that people never get what they want, not even what they deserve – good or bad. How many times had I heard Kenny say "Wish in one hand and shit in the other. See which fills up faster"? I had never been much good at connecting the things I wanted with how to go about getting them.

It was at this moment – as I sat at the breakfast

nook in the home of surely blameless people and smoked two of Kenny Fortuna's Lucky Strikes, his disgusting snores echoing, even above the now-booming thunder – I realized, maybe for the first time, how much I loved my parents, how I was of them, inseparable. Then I heard another round of crackling *ack-ack* from Kenny, and I determined I would march back down those sweet, piney, blond step-treads and silence him once and for all.

He was dead out, inside the fireplace on the firebrick hearth he had laid that morning. I picked up the empty Meadow Gold carton. The smell of whiskey, some kind of booze, in his buttermilk. I nudged him with a boot. Like kicking a sack of mortar. He didn't move, just his chest, up and down, as that roaring bellows in his craw spat fire, and drops of rain hissed about him as they sluiced down the chimney and leaked through the terra cotta flue.

I stepped outside and fetched the chain and lock that anchored the mixer. When I returned, I nudged Kenny. He remained comatose, rumbling phlegm. I wrapped the chain three times around his waist, twice around his neck, looped it through the cast iron hole in the damper's control arm, allowing not even a link of slack, engaged the padlock shackle, which clicked audibly, removed the key, and dropped it in my pocket. Still he didn't stir.

I picked up Kenny's huge trowel and sliced it through the black mortar on his board. It had stiffened, but quickly freshened with water from the tempering can into the rich grainy consistency of *polenta*.

I had never laid brick, yet erecting a wall seemed completely natural, instinctive, yet vaguely connected to a kind of fear. Maybe what my mother feared – that thing in her that made getting back at people, taking vengeance, building a wall of silence, so seductive. The desire to murder things. Darkness had already come on. Lightning fizzed. Thunder tolled; it had crossed the river. Still it rained, though not as fiercely.

Mimicking Shotty, I mounted at the mouth of the fireplace the first courses of red antique bricks I'd earlier stocked for Kenny, a dozen bricks per course, slicking mortar onto their faces and heels, like icing a cake, canting just so, tamping them down with the trowel handle, using Kenny's brick hammer to bust in half the bricks I used on either terminus, moving the plumb line up with each course. Kenny never stirred, just throttled along like a massive V-8 badly out of tune.

I stepped out onto the little porch for another bucket of mud. A jagged drizzle fell. Fog rolled in. Lights from faraway houses twitched in the murk. I reentered the cellar and worked steadily. After the tenth course, I could no longer see Kenny's body – just his face, and the gold *P* on his cap catching the cellar light. I laid the eleventh course, then the twelfth and thirteenth. Kenny was now invisible. The only evidence that he was there, just inches from me, was his guttural, inebriated snore that only further fueled my loathing for him and made me hasten. I finished the fourteenth, laid the first brick in the final course, the fifteenth, and was progressing along the row when I heard voices – maybe the people who owned the place bringing in more of their stuff. But it was Kenny – the snoring had ceased – talking in his sleep. A jumble of syllables I couldn't make out at first, but then: *"O my God, I am heartily sorry for having offended Thee . . . ."* He was reciting *The Act of Contrition.*

He sounded sober as a judge. Maybe he wasn't talking in his sleep. When I turned back to the wall, there was Kenny's face – his eyes, a few strands of white hair that had fallen out of his cap – in that remaining rectangle, the size of a number ten envelope, awaiting the final brick. The cavity glowed, as if emanating from him was an aura, perhaps the light my father seemed able to detect even in awful people – what he surely saw in my mother, even at her worst. But, of course, it could have only been the glow from the quartz in the firebrick ignited by the lightning leaking down the flue.

As I stood there, Kenny's hand snaked through the remaining space into the cellar. Like in a horror movie or a grisly miracle in Butler's *Lives of the Saints* – holy and unholy at once – and it nearly knocked me over. His hand flailed eerily, searching for something. Just that hand, his Biblical right hand, his brick hand, his fist-hand. His brutalized, enormous, sorrowful gray hand. "Come closer," he said, his voice subdued, gentle.

I moved toward the hand. "Say it with me," Kenny said softly. "*. . . and I detest all my sins because of Thy just punishments,*" he continued and, reflexively, I joined him: "*but most of all because they offend Thee, my God, Who art all-good and deserving of all my love.*"

Suddenly, the hand lurched, raking my face. Kenny's enormous fingers gouged into my mouth, clenching my teeth, suffocating me, his thumb digging into my chin, inching toward my windpipe, as he wrenched and pulled and growled. I felt my mandible separate from my skull, the ungodly well of power Kenny Fortuna embodied. Nothing was clear – that he was evil, that he was a child of God. His soul remained invisible. In his hand, gagging me, that tasted so clearly of revenge, my jaw was coming away. I bit down on his stony, calloused fingers until I tasted blood, and finally he released me.

Then he laughed and laughed – that grimy engine, those cracked head gaskets. "You think that's how you brick a wall, Matilda? Just line them up like Tinker Toys? I'll come right through this jackleg piece of shit and rip your fucking head off." He pulled in his bleeding hand and punched the wall. "But if you have one ball in your body – if there's even half a fucking ball between you and your old man – you better leave me in here." He punched the wall again. "But you won't, Matilda." Another punch. "You're too much of a coward, too much your old man's kid, too much Rita the *puttana's* little pig-shit Irish bastard, to leave me – even though you know, that when you let me out, I'll beat you bloody. I'll kill you. And that's what you'll do: you'll tear down this wall and unchain me. You know that's what you're going to do, you fucking little faggot, and then I'll kill you. It's already come to pass, Matilda." Kenny laughed and pummeled the wall – a dull, furious thud. The chain rang each time he jabbed the quaking wall.

Then he returned to *The Act of Contrition*, shouting: *"I firmly resolve with the help of Thy grace, to sin no more and to avoid the near occasion of sin."* I joined him again as he recited it, doubling, tripling him in volume. I screamed and screamed and screamed until finally he shut up, yet the chain continued to vibrate.

I dipped into the black mortar and troweled it on the final brick. Light trickled from his chamber.

Claire as the Blessed Mother

(After the painting, *Madonna and Child with Two Angels,* by Francesco Francia)

Of all the girls, Claire Raffo radiates that wistful Italian Renaissance gaze, the aching Madonna piety: chaste mouth, hooded almond eyes, flawless complexion, a luminous, stained-glass iconography that murmurs tragically from within.

But there's also that unmistakable, embarrassed smirk, the boredom those Italian girls from East Liberty, when forced to pose, affect. Claire isn't one of the hard ones. She doesn't brawl or carry a switchblade. Cloaked in the detached fearlessness of Tallulah Bankhead in *Lifeboat*, she's extemporaneously brilliant, the class's electrifying intellect, and wields profanity like someone of great wealth.

Claire has hidden in her purse, along with a pack of Kools, Sylvia Plath's *Ariel* and *The Bell Jar.* She's intoxicated by Plath's foreboding poems and stunning death, her husky brogue nudging from the other realm. Like something out of Butler's *Lives of the Saints.*

If our teacher, Sister John, who favors Plath, beyond beauty – Carroll Baker in *The Miracle* – discovers these volumes, much less the cigarettes, and who knows what else – Claire keeps a journal – there will be a call to the Raffos' home, and Claire, along with her parents, will be summoned to the convent Sunday after 10:30 Mass. Mrs. Raffo, like my mother – they know each other – won't take even this much shit from a nun. Claire loves her mother and hates her tyrant landscape gardener father: Walt (Gualtiero Raffo). Despite his revenant, cave man demeanor, colossal girth, and minotaur head, he'd grovel before exquisite John like a whipped cur – fedora in hand, necktie to his stubbly chin – and swear his daughter and those dirty books and cigarettes *anathema*. Mrs. Raffo would detonate. There would be a scene.

The book Sister John assigned the girls is *Pride and Prejudice*. Claire is especially intrigued with the novel's treatment of the epic divide between marrying for love and marrying for position; the latter she equates with the most insipid complacency. Manners are critical, of course, but sometimes you have to tell people off. Not at all lost on her is the screaming irony that Sister John, a nun, with her vow of chastity, holds forth on romantic love and marriage: seduction; consummation; entwined naked bodies. The eighth-grade boys, on the other hand – we still bray like donkeys – read *Robinson Crusoe*. Its cannibalism thrills me.

Regrettably, Claire has fallen for Allen Compton, an older boy in high school at Peabody, about to drop out, a blackguard, a real *gavone* – in truth an apprentice assassin, all black leather, the aftermath of *West Side Story*, without the music, without the poetry. She'll reckon much later the horror of Compton; but, by then, it will be too late, and I'll be in the picture. Five years from now, 1972 – the summer she tries to break it off with Compton and he insists she belongs to him, that he will never permit her to leave him – she and I meet on a fire escape at a party, by happenstance on the Feast of the Assumption. Hovering the bed we'll share at Claire's apartment are lines from Plath's "Lady Lazarus" that she painted red on her ceiling: "Out of the ash / I rise with my red hair / and I eat men like air." At this moment, however, 1967, Claire, the Blessed Mother, is not aware I exist. Does not know my name. I did not get a part in the play. Nevertheless, albeit not for a long time, I will be the next boy to complicate her life.

Claire as Mary – almost a joke, a satire only she is aware of – but she admires how she looks in the costume: velvet and silk brocade robes and *gonnelle* – cobalt, incarnadine, emerald. The white *camicia* that peeks from her left sleeve. The lace headdress beneath the veil. Melodramatic cascades of fabric. The golden nimbus affixed to her head – cardboard, yes, but it floats above her of its own accord. There is also decided cachet in being the Mother of God, chosen above all others. Angelically, Sister John, no angel, except for her face and hands, all you can see of her, plays the harp and sings *Regina Coeli* in her unearthly soprano – so haunting, crows in the May sycamores just beyond the sash turn ash and a sudden wind whips up.

Claire adores the Christ Child, but knows what's coming. She's studied it in the Gospels. One unthinkable Friday, thirty-three years down the road, she'll keep vigil at the foot of the cross as spongy, carnal, blond Yeshua, the Jewish infant on her lap, falsely accused, then tortured – a put-up job by the State – is executed by crucifixion. Despite the hard times ahead, Claire loves having the naked Prince of Peace in her lap, a flame-orange chaplet looped around his neck. A real baby, obviously a child from the neighborhood whose mother donated him for this occasion. It's clear He's a born iconoclast, androgynous, already composing *The Beatitudes.* That raised right hand: Is it Benediction? Reprimand? It won't be long before the baby fat burns off and He's lean, hard as a hammer – *a thief in the night* – His open palm clenched in the righteous fist of revolution.

The blue-winged angels attending Claire are Nicolina Russo and Davida Pofi, Claire's bodyguards and best friends – two girls not to trifle with – also chosen for their looks. They whisper, during the play, as if no one notices. Inside her black habit, Sister John reads their minds. After the play, they've schemed to meet Junior Rancatore and Joe Brush in Junior's pink Chevy II and catch *Bonnie and Clyde* at Silver Lake, a drive-in under the Larimer Bridge, on Washington Boulevard. They don't get to have haloes.

Sister John designed the set. Inspired by a vision of the hereafter, she painted, in a trance, its unimaginable estate on bedsheets: shimmering trees, luscious lawns – like the vast gardens Claire's father frets over and makes so beautiful for the rich in Highland Park and Fox Chapel – the legendary Biblical firmament, atop it the *della robbia* sky – the vaults of Heaven and some pretty little clouds, cumulonimbi, not bothering a soul, into which Claire, the Madonna, exempt from death, will one day be assumed.

A Story of Glass

Keith, the sweetest guy on earth, was bitter, feeling worthless. He had taken to getting a little too fucked up, and I suppose I just let it go – the way you let it go when someone's your old friend, your best friend, and he's been having a hard time, and you feel like you don't know enough yourself to tell him to slow down or lighten up.

He'd been drinking whiskey and was driving way too fast down Penn Avenue towards the block where he and Bonnie had had the apartment above the flower shop, same block as Saint Lawrence O'Toole Church, across the street from The Little Sisters of the Poor convent.

Along Penn were streetcar tracks gashed into cobblestones, patches of ice and snow, a nasty February wind. He hit one of those trolley rails funny – treacherous even in nice weather – and we took off like the car was on skis, totally out of control, skidded through the red light, just missed a telephone pole, and, *boom*, destroyed both passenger tires and rims on the high curb at Atlantic and Penn, right in front of Tootie's – everything in an instant – the windshield mysteriously shattered.

We were in Keith's dad's '66 green Plymouth Satellite, no doubt a sporty car in its day, still solid enough, but feeble shocks and rusting out. I liked Keith's dad, Mr. Gentile, a steelworker at Mesta, down along the

Monongahela. I liked Mrs. Gentile, too. She worked in the lunchroom at Fulton School. Keith had good parents, but he'd been testing them a little too much, pushing their endurance beyond what was reasonable. After the abortion, everything was up in the air with Keith and Bonnie. They had both returned home to their parents and hadn't seen each other for a month.

Still running, the radio playing "Oh, Girl," by the Chi-Lites, the car was jacked at a pretty good angle up on the curb. We squinted through the prismed glass at a million apparitions – and laughed. Keith turned off the juice, and we slid down out to the street. We didn't say anything, didn't check to see if we were okay, just headed for Tootie's, ten feet away, as if that had been our destination all along. The big, heavy traffic light there at the corner swayed wildly in the wind. The lights were on in the convent. The icon of Saint Lawrence O'Toole on the front of church was bathed in floodlights. Not a single car abroad.

Tootie's was a diner, a chrome caboose. The menu was written on a board above the grill: no-nonsense Pittsburgh food. Nothing fancy, just good as hell, and you never got tired of it. Franco Harris, the famous Steelers running back, lived in the neighborhood. An autographed picture of him hung on the wall: the Immaculate Reception shot where he's hallucinating because the football has appeared in his hands out of thin air, and he's charging like a bull for the goal line.

Keith, Bonnie, and I had been in Tootie's one night in the summer – before Bonnie got pregnant, before Keith flunked out of college – and Franco walked in with Frenchy Fuqua, another Steeler. Franco was inconspicuous, but he was Franco, so there it is. But Frenchy, whose nickname was The Count, wore a superfly cape and platforms with – honest to God –

goldfish swimming in the massive heels. Keith and Bonnie had been so happy together that night, wholly in love, twined around each other. They planned to marry.

Keith and I perched on stools at the long counter, grateful for the warmth and good light. A shelf with bowling and softball trophies ran the length of the wall. There was a jukebox, but this was not the night for a jukebox. At the grill, the cook – a great big bald guy with a fringe of black hair tangled around his head, and an immense white shirt and apron – kept his back to the counter. His arms moved gruffly as he cooked. He never turned. Two guys ate down the counter from us, and that was it.

A very young woman, but older than us, walked right out of *Petrified Forest* wearing Bette Davis's wavy light brown hair and pink waitress frock. Stitched above her heart in white script was her name: *Billie.* She said to no one in particular: "You're going to need a tow truck."

"The car's okay," Keith said – in his Army jacket and bell-bottoms, his jointless noodle body and crazy Sputnik hair.

"I see," she said. "May I take your order?"

We each got a couple cuts of pizza to limber up, while we decided what to have. It was late. Billie hadn't expected a couple of rubes – that she'd have never given the time of day – to blow in out of such a miserable night, after wrecking their car at her threshold. The wind howled. Tootie's shimmied. She wanted to go home.

Billie listened intently as we ordered, and nodded as she wrote everything down. I got what I always got, a meatball sandwich; Keith, what he always got, a hot sausage sandwich. She smiled at us after she took our order, slapped it down at the cook's elbow, and he went to work. Hairy, powerful arms snaked out with knives and forks and ladles, his back to us like a priest, at the altar, putting together the recipe. He had sweated all the way through his apron.

Nobody said anything. I had a cigarette. Keith had three. The cook smoked, too. Every few beats, he reached for his cigarette, smoldering in an ashtray on a ledge above him, left it in his mouth another few beats while he worked, then set it back in the ashtray. Billie didn't smoke. She stood just a few feet away on the other side of the counter reading *Slaughterhouse-Five.* Her hair in that nice light, and the darkness outside was a little too much.

The cook dished up the food. Billie grabbed a napkin out of a dispenser to mark her place and laid the book on the counter. She placed two plates and our tickets in front of us.

"Where'd you get the name Billie?" Keith asked.

"What are you going to do about the car?" she countered.

"The car's fine," Keith said, a cigarette, his fifth, twitching in his hand.

The towering cook turned and said, "If it's fine, how about you driving it off my sidewalk?" He had a sad moon face. His apron, stitched with his name, *Eugene*, was splashed with the night.

The two guys at the counter split.

Keith and I weren't fighters. Our only credentials were stupidity.

"Where'd you get the name Billie?" Keith asked again.

The cook hadn't moved. His question still hung in the smoky fluorescence.

Billie stepped in front of Eugene. He made two

of her. She placed both palms on the counter in front of Keith. Her uniform sleeves had white French cuffs, with emerald cuff links. "Because it's short for William," she said, then asked, "Now what are you going to do about that car?"

"The car's okay," Keith said – in the falsetto he defaulted to when he got worked up. That madhouse wire head of his. He listened to voices from other planets. He took advice from aliens.

"I don't just want your asses out the door," Eugene said. "I want that piece of shit off my curb, or I'll call the cops. In the meantime, pay up and get the hell out of here."

"That's my dad's car," Keith said.

Maybe Billie was Eugene's daughter. They didn't look alike, but you don't always look like your father. Neither of them had been there the night I'd been in with Keith and Bonnie.

We threw some money on the counter and walked out to the dead car. The way those busted wheels had folded at such a painful angle, like broken legs, the axles had to have ruptured.

"What should we do?" Keith asked.

I said nothing.

"My dad's going to shit his pants. I mean – I'm killing my parents with all this Bonnie shit already. I flunked the fuck out of school." Keith kind of cried, but I was okay with it. I didn't have great prospects either. He reached for his smokes and couldn't find them. He apoplectically patted every pocket, over and over. He looked like a bird blasted out of the sky.

I put my arm around Keith. "Let's walk a little, man, and figure this out. It'll be okay."

We headed toward the church, past the flower shop. Someone had moved into Keith and Bonnie's apartment. A faint glow lit their lone second-storey window. The lights in the convent had extinguished. Saint Lawrence O'Toole still gleamed in agony from his perch. Sirens screamed.

"You think that guy at Tootie's called the cops?" Keith asked.

"Nah, I bet he didn't."

The flower shop windows were faintly lit, foreboding, funereal, the doldrum of late winter flowers – faded gladiolas and dish gardens, the bitter cud that everything is illusion and sorrow. Spring was so far away and lost, it might never return. The avenue was abandoned, tired of it all, nothing but sirens and *Who-gives-a-fuck*.

Keith stared up at the apartment window. It flickered – candlelight.

"Let's keep walking," I said.

"I'm going to take Billie some flowers."

Lights blinked on in the convent. It started snowing hard.

"The nuns woke up," said Keith said, in the falsetto. Tears rolled down his beatific face.

He wore heavy harness boots. The flower shop window, an entire story of glass, withstood his first two kicks. Then it cascaded down, like ice and bells, plates and spalls, shrouding Keith in a fantastic caul of lethal glass – as if he were this average stiff in a Marvel comic book, beset by trouble and disgrace, who one frozen night traipses into catastrophe, and finds himself transformed, mutated, and becomes another being.

For a moment, I couldn't make him out in that blinding hail of snow and glass, the jagged rays of every light on Penn Avenue enveloping him. It fell and fell. There was no end to it. Then it ceased, as abruptly as the Satellite had in front of Tootie's – and there stood Keith, glowing, unscathed. A chaplet of glass flickered in his insane hair.

He walked into the flower shop display and seized a handful of crimson gladiolas and a withered tangle of baby's breath. Clutching his bouquet, he strode back down Penn Avenue towards Tootie's and his father's car.

The *Malocchio*

At the height of her obsession with the evil eye – the eyes, she called it, the *malocchio* – my mother, desperate to get pregnant, arranged an audience with Grazziella and insisted I accompany her.

Half-witch, half-holy woman, handed down, generation to generation – like a curse, like a precious icon, a splinter from the true cross – Grazziella lived on the poor end of Shakespeare Street in an Insulbrick shack with a chimney that coughed smoke year-round. Pittsburgh's Urban Renewal Project had bulldozed every home and tree in that end of East Liberty. Nothing but brick piles and twisted metal peeked above the mud lots hacked with maudlin footprints and toppled clotheslines – trampled dresses and diapers yet clinging to them. Jackhammers still throttled. The stench of gasoline cloaked the ether – and in the distance, from Penn Avenue, rose the heavenly aroma of Nabisco's ovens. Like an anomalous eye, in the midst of the demolition, Grazziella's house slouched, somehow spared by the wrecking ball. Out of her soot yard swooned a near-dead buckeye tree.

I had gone once with my friends to throw buckeyes off her tin roof, careful to stay far enough away from her telescopic gaze when she appeared at the door and unleashed bolts of Napolitano invective as we hid in the bushes and laughed. My laughter, however, was feigned.

Grazziella terrified me. The others did not seem to see the dress of white smoke she wore, a wedding gown stitched with pearls and lace doves – gardenias and cobwebs adorning her hair – not so much white, but the faded yellow of ancient book stock.

Even back when my mother had been a little girl, Grazziella haunted East Liberty with her insatiable widowhood. Her husband, Lorenzo, a fruit merchant, had purchased the neighborhood's first automobile. My mother didn't know when exactly – 1926, maybe '27. She hadn't been born yet.

"Hearsay, Rita," my father said, glancing at her over his newspaper. "The glorious myths of your childhood."

She told him to go to hell. He smiled and returned to the *Post-Gazette.*

On a fair May 1st morning, one of Our Lady's high feast days, whatever year it had been – my mother, as she told the story, shot my father a murderous look – Lorenzo left home in his gleaming roadster to drive to his produce business downtown where the railroad cars crept along the dock sidings with grapes and lemons and artichokes from California. A freak blizzard had whipped up, and Lorenzo was massacred when his new Ford skidded in front of a streetcar on Liberty Avenue.

In the wake of Lorenzo's death, Grazziella destroyed every dish, curio, and sacred object in her trousseau, then donned her wedding dress. From that day forward, she wore white to mark her devastation – not the traditional spider black of the Italian widow. She took to a wheelchair and became a cripple, though she could be seen walking among her zinnias, collecting bees in jars for sooth and sortilege. No child would venture into her yard to retrieve an errant ball. Disappeared pets were said to have been eaten by Grazziella. In the garden, beneath her crop of Romas, lurked a graveyard filled with kidnapped children. Lorenzo had not been remanded to the sacred dirt of Mount Carmel Cemetery; Grazziella had salted him down, like *soppresatta*, and he reposed within the walls of her jittering house.

My father's eyes, as he listened to my mother's account, never drifted from the newspaper; but he couldn't stop smirking.

"Travis, you bastard," my mother hissed, then spun out of the room, her indignation hatching silence, like a thorn bush, throughout the house.

My mother, for some reason desperate to have a baby, was convinced that someone had put the eyes on her, the *malocchio*, and that was why she couldn't conceive. My father had urged her to visit the doctor, but she refused. There wasn't a thing wrong with her body. She hadn't had a speck of trouble getting knocked up with me, she taunted him. She had been cursed. That's why she couldn't have a baby. A caul of vendetta had been cast over her.

At my mother's announcement that she was going to Grazziella, my father had laughed: "Jesus Christ, Rita. We live in a city renowned for medicine, and you've made an appointment with that crazy old *strega* to read tea leaves and throw bones on the floor."

After knocking on Grazziella's warped door, my mother and I waited a long time. When Graziella appeared, my mother kissed her hand like Grazziella was the Pope; intoned breathily, *Grazziella*; and handed her the two-pound box of Russell Stover chocolates and the carton of Chesterfields we'd brought as homage.

I shaded myself behind my mother, but the ancient woman pointed a crooked finger between my eyes and said, "I know this one."

I said nothing, yet felt my insides coil. I knew

not to look in her eyes, the color of a skink's tail. She motioned us into the kitchen, which reeked with the brackish vapor of *broccoli rabe* brewing on the stove. On the walls blazed portraits of mutilated saints, sick boxes, shelved jars of herbs and unguents.

"Why have you come to see me?" Grazziella asked.

"Someone is punishing me," my mother said.

Grazziella inclined her head gravely and raised a silver eyebrow.

We sat at her kitchen table – strewn with Italian newspapers – she in a rattan wheelchair, lighting cigarette after cigarette, holding each puff a long while, then lifting her runneled, gray face to the ceiling to slowly exhale.

Opening the box of candy, she pointed to a dark-chocolate fluted rectangle and pronounced, "Vanilla Cream." She nibbled it, displayed the vanilla cream center, then guzzled it. A dozen more times she predicted what was hidden by the gorgeous sheen of chocolate, each time greedily gobbling the candy until she came to a domed chocolate and pronounced, "Cordial cherry. *Mangiare*."

How could she have known that cordial cherries were my favorite? I smiled. It was a candy I loved above all others. My ritual was to first skive the dome off, suck until it melted, then drink the milky, cordial cherry juice, before devouring the entire cherry in its tiny chocolate cup. The stories my father had scoffed at were true. Grazziella possessed supernatural powers. She had read my mind.

I plucked the chocolate from the box and brought it to my mouth. Its scent intoxicated me – in fact, lured me from my body for an instant. I floated above my mother, her palm in Grazziella's parchment hands, their eyes closed as they whispered. Then I bit into it.

I was seized with unbearable pain. I pried the cordial cherry from my mouth. Secreted within its chocolate robe had not been a cherry at all, but a buckeye, its mahogany finish inscribed with my two front teeth.

ACID

Keith Gentile and I are thumbing into Wheeling from California, PA, a little coal-mining town along the grimy Monongahela River – Keith, among other things, is flunking out of a little college there – when a big white Ford Econoline van slows, coasts past us, and parks fifty yards up the washed-out shoulder. After a week of blizzards, it's been raining with plague vengeance. We sprint after the van, fenders of water parting as we run. A side door swings open, and we roll into it. No seats. Carpet covers the floor. Nice and warm, there are lit votive candles stationed here and there.

Keith and I feel lucky to have copped a ride in this monsoon. But the occupants of the van are midgets. Like the guys on Studio Wrestling. Blocky and muscular, a set of pecs on a belt buckle. Long hair and beards. I've never met one, and I know Keith hasn't either.

Nobody but the driver, Mack, really speaks at first: the usual *where you from, where you headed?* The van is rigged to accommodate his stature: a big high seat so he can peer over the dashboard, brake and throttle on an elevated platform his feet can reach. Marty, the guy riding shotgun, turns and looks at us the whole time. Everyone else – all midgets – sitting or lying on the floor, nod in greeting. Very serious, but friendly enough. Some sleep. A few get up and walk around.

They're short enough to not ding their heads on the van's ceiling.

There was a time when Keith and I would have cracked up, laughed like little kids in church. We have long careers in undistinguished behavior. *Jesus Christ, a vanful of midgets!* But, tonight, there's no laugh in us. We're glad to have landed in such a mellow space on such a bad night – and Keith, who can be like some wild thing out there, needs to be handled with kid gloves.

Mack says they're headed for Wheeling, too. Asks if we know where the whorehouses are. Neither Keith nor I have ever been to a whorehouse. Back in high school, not that long ago at all – last year – we tagged along with some other guys and got as far as the parlor in a whorehouse underneath the Homestead High Level Bridge. Then we chickened out. Marty says there's supposed to be one in Wheeling where the girls are all dwarves, no shit. That's the one they're looking for. I think he's goofing around, so I just laugh.

"Square business," Marty says. "I'm not kidding."

"Maybe you'd like to have a go with a dwarf," Mack suggests.

Keith tells him he's engaged, so he can't have a go with anybody. His girl, back in Pittsburgh, is pregnant, and he plans to marry her.

"How about you then?" Marty nods toward me. "You up for that Wheeling feeling?"

I tell him I don't know, but of course I have no interest in such a thing. He and Mack laugh.

Then, like they're reading my mind, they give a spiel about the differences between midgets and dwarves. Midgets are simply miniature versions of regular people. It's a matter of proportions. Midgets are scaled-down homo sapiens, like someone bathed them in the shrink ray. Dwarves, on the other hand, possess abnormal body proportions: biggish heads, truncated limbs. They're skilled artificers and craftsmen, noted for legendary strength. They want to make sure that we know we're in a van full of dwarves – not midgets.

"Mack can lift a Shetland pony," Marty confides. Mack confirms this with a sober nod. "The actual munchkins in *The Wizard of Oz*. Some are dwarves, some midgets. Check it out next time it's on."

The dwarves in the van are dressed in normal clothes, but I keep picturing them in chain mail, little broadswords and helmets, etc. Like Gimli and Ori and Nori and the rest of them in *The Hobbit*. I'm worried I'm going to start laughing and, what's more, I feel Keith sending out his signature shrill vibe. He's struggling mightily to not let go with a frantic laughing jag – which would turn into some freak-out requiring hospitalization. But then we both calm down and, through telepathic powers old friends possess – we were born nearly the same minute at Pittsburgh Hospital – agree not to look at each other.

It's late, the early hours of the morning, rain pounding down on the road's omniscient hush. The dwarves bed down, blow out all but one candle. Mack and Marty, turned to the road for the duration, pop into the tape deck something I don't recognize. It might be chanting. Medieval woodwinds. It's nice and warm in the van, and the music's very soothing. Keith and I, completely soaked, settle into a pile of blankets in a corner. The others sleep. They snore like it's scripted, and their beards luff up in the wind-drift of their heavy exhales like the dwarves in *Snow White*.

I think we pass into West Virginia – Keith and I are going to celebrate a little down there, get his mind off things – the legal drinking age is eighteen – when my head knocks off something hard as I angle into those blankets. So, I pull back the blankets. There's just this last tiny flame on the white votive wick. But I know what a gun looks like. Not just one, but more and more as I inch back the blankets: shotguns and machine guns and pistols. An entire arsenal. Dope, too. Bricks and bricks of Mary Jane and countless big clear baggies of white powder. I decide not to wake Keith, but he's right there at my elbow gaping.

"Jesus Christ, Fritzy," he hisses. "Jesus Christ."

Keith is not a murderer, but he could reach for a gun. I cover the stuff back up and whisper, "Just keep cool. Okay?"

"Keep cool," he mutters. "Keep cool. Keep cool." He lies back down and pulls a blanket over his head, reciting, "Keep cool." The blanket pulses with his inevitable detonation.

From the tape deck, flutes rustle like wind. Our tires slish across the deserted highway. The barely guttering candle flame solemnly laps the glass it sits in. The dwarves slumber. Dangerously sad. Like all has been lost. Mythic. These guys are from another world. They have guns, and they're running dope, and it's up to me to do something about it – to save Keith and me. To save the world. But I don't know what to do, and I'm not even sure what side I'm on.

There's an explosion, and the dwarves come out of their blankets. Like Judgment Day. As if they have the drill down pat. Keith sits up – like in a Poe story. Someone has dropped a bomb on us or maybe broadsided us with a bazooka. Mack fights the wheel. We're going sideways. Marty's yelling "Jesus Christ, hold on" at Mack. The van convulses. There's the decided stench of incineration. In a twirl, we may be on fire.

The dwarves keen like a Greek chorus. Like the explosion was their cue. Like they know exactly what's happening – what's hit us: what they've expected all along. The stakes are that high: the guns and dope. It all comes clear in that instant – that they're part of something. Keith hasn't moved. Just sits there like rigor mortis as we spin and spin off the road into oblivion.

Mack gets us to the shoulder. Marty turns and says, "It's a blowout. Front right tire." But the dwarves screech so loudly they don't hear. At that moment, a Pennsylvania Highway Patrolman pulls up behind us, hazards flailing. Keith starts to quicken. He's coming back to life. Through the van's rear window, the trooper walks through the rain toward us – coming into relief, bigger and bigger, against the sodden dawn.

"Shut the fuck up," Mack screams at his buddies. And suddenly there is absolute silence, as the trooper reaches Mack's open window, takes one look at him, then switches on a gargantuan flashlight and peers into the back of the van.

With that searchlight in my eyes, I can't see a thing, but I chance a look at Keith. He smiles; his mouth unseals. Then he laughs. Louder and louder, demonically, like he's finally gone over: knocking up Bonnie, flunking out, the dwarves, and the guns and dope, the blown tire, and now the law. Sometimes it's too fucking much.

The trooper digs his light into Keith, bathing him in technicolor caricature. Keith like a crazy-ass super villain experiencing some kind of fanatic conversion, stumbling upon what it's really all about. Like Saint Paul: transmission zapped, electrical system exponentially shorted. Right there: Keith snaps, and I witness it. It's all I can do to hang on myself.

That long cone of the trooper's white light. Keith swallows it – the light itself, that abyss of concentrated incandescence. Scarfs the entire scene – like it's his last meal. Down his throat, in the caverns of his guts, dwarves caper toward their weapons. Votive fires ignite. Sirens lift from the land, a regiment of hallucinatory lights on the backs of state cruisers arrived to shoot it out with us. I see the whole world inside Keith. Entire armies march.

The Day John Wayne Died

On a Sunday, my parents' only day off from their nocturnal restaurant jobs, the three of us walked to the Sheridan Square on Penn Avenue and caught the afternoon matinee of *The Alamo.* It was 1960. Mere days earlier, John Kennedy had narrowly defeated Richard Nixon, whom my parents despised, to become the United States' youngest and first Catholic president. Kennedy's French wife, Jackie, was thirty-one, exotically pretty, and eight months pregnant. The Kennedys also had a nearly three-year-old daughter named Caroline. She and I were contemporaries; I dreamed of meeting her. My mother dreamed of having another baby.

Pittsburgh still swooned over Bill Mazeroski's epic home run to clinch the World Series for the Pirates over the mythic New York Yankees a month earlier. The last jubilant flecks of confetti and ticker tape blew about the city – and now Kennedy on top of it. Dynasties had toppled: first the bully Yankees, then the bully Nixon. Kennedy vowed to take America to the moon.

My mother held tightly to my hand, though I would have walked obediently beside her without the tether. The shopping district of East Liberty was packed with holiday shoppers. We passed beggars and the blind, the halt and lame. From their stations on the sidewalk, they dangled tin cups, into which people, including my parents, dropped pennies and sometimes nickels and dimes. The blind offered pencils in return, but my parents politely declined. My mother believed that anything accepted from these people would generate disease.

As we strolled to the movies that pretty, mild, cloudless November sabbath, five days from Thanksgiving, hope – laced with smoke and ore dust from the heaving steel mills along the rivers – hovered the city. The next day, city workers would drape glorious Christmas garlands across Penn Avenue. The future had arrived and, though my parents and I basked in its earliest moments, it would soon become apparent that no one had prepared for it.

We paid the woman in her glass ticket booth, entered the Sheridan, and bought buttered popcorn and Reymer's Lemon Blend. The theater was churchlike: the dark, on-tiptoe hush; the settling of bodies; tiny slashes of illumination, like votives, on the aisle seats; ushers with epaulets and flashlights; the immense blank screen like an altar the instant before the priest – regaled in Birettum and sacred vestments, in his left hand the chalice and veil – emerged from the sacristy into the sanctuary to ignite the sacrifice of the Mass.

Suddenly the screen burst into light. Porky and Petunia Pig, accompanied by a goofy riff of brass, piano, and xylophone, capered across it. Two minutes and forty-six seconds later, after Porky stuttered "That's all, folks," Paul Francis Webster's "The Green Leaves of Summer," scored mournfully by Dimitri Tiomkin, piped through the Sheridan its Moorish bugle call, *El Deguello*, and there was no going back.

I was ignorant of the recorded history of the Alamo, an old mission in Texas originally named for St. Anthony of Padua, the patron saint of lost things, where for thirteen days in the winter of 1836, a band of 180 rebels, seeking independence from Mexico, held out against Generalissimo Antonio de Padua María Severino López de Santa Anna y Pérez de Lebrón and his army of 4000, until the last among them was slaughtered. The opening film credits flashed across the face of the actual Alamo. Upon its ramparts, a toppled cross had transposed into a massive X.

The movie was typically quixotic, filled with restorative moments of comic relief, horses and swagger, guns and panoramic glory – so different from the life I sat inside, between my parents, Travis and Rita Sweeney. As the story took shape, the odds against the men in the Alamo mounted. But trouble guaranteed an authentic story: there was bound to be bloodshed and death. The good and right thing, however – perhaps we might even call it rectitude – would inevitably triumph. It's what I had come to expect from the world of stories that protected me.

Santa Anna's troops appeared expendable. Their humorless, mechanized anonymity and tin soldier uniforms doomed them. And, of course, there were the stars: Richard Widmark, as Jim Bowie; Laurence Harvey, as William Travis (my father's first name was Travis); and John Wayne, as Davy Crockett, whose buckskin and coonskin cap alone guaranteed things in the long run would play out fine. At the time, I hadn't known any sad stories, even though my own story strayed into dismal, but I had neither language nor paradigm for *the tragic* that day, and for that I'm grateful.

My parents neither subscribed to an abiding order that governed the universe nor put much stock in happy endings. My mother maintained a grudging belief in God, and my dad was essentially a nonbeliever. He found religion and churchgoing in particular irrelevant. A student of history, he had known empirically how the movie would end; there was, indeed, but one ending. In fact, I'd wager he believed in history more than anything: that the most predictable thing is that things remain unpredictable. He didn't require the fantasy, the story, that religion provided. He trafficked in facts, documents. He loved the newspaper.

My mother, however, desired the kind of optimism, the often thoroughly unrealistic cosmos, that stories tended toward, and I suppose I was more like her in that sense. My dad had given up hope of being rescued and had learned to enjoy the moment, while she thrashed desperately about the patch of earth she spent her life on, stalled between falsehood and fact. Mired in the capricious vaults of memory – by turns compassionate and murderous – what *really* happened at a precise moment in time, scrivened on the palimpsest of eternity – birth, death, an argument, a missed opportunity, a glance, faulty aim – becomes as malleable as dough: *what she said, what he said, who's a son of a bitch.*

The plight of the rebels grew dire, then direr. Their women and children, also holed up in the mission, were evacuated. Then came the inevitable siege. Mexican troops spidered up crude ladders and over the Alamo walls. I hated them as I watched the men I had come to know and love swarmed. Shot and bayoneted, blown from the parapets – the mission ablaze, its walls powdered by cannonade – they fell one by one, in protracted, agonized, bloody pirouettes. My mother held her hands over her face. My father looked straight ahead. They had forgotten me. The theater seemed on the verge of lift-off – a B-52 on its last bomb run.

The Alamo was the first John Wayne picture I'd ever seen, yet his face was familiar, but where had I seen it? Perhaps in a dream, or perhaps in one of my mother's. She and I often wandered each other's dreams.

John Wayne was an archetype, every bit as invulnerable as Kennedy and Mazeroski. He couldn't be killed.

He swatted away charging infidels with a Kentucky long-rifle and a flaming torch. His shirt was blue. A powder horn and Bowie knife depended from his belt. Santa Anna's foppish troops fell in his wake like puppets. As he leapt across a patch of dead men and horses, a Mexican soldier thrust a lance through his side, skewering him to a plank door. Arterial blood erupted onto Wayne's vest and britches. He'd lost his rifle, but swept away his assailant with the torch, gripped the lance with his free hand, snapped it off at his belt and staggered through the jamb. The bloody shaft of the lance spiked from the door. His back smeared with gore. He lurched to the threshold of the powder magazine and flung the torch among the kegs. Its flaming tongue waxed yellow among them for a long time – until the powder detonated, the walls imploded, and everything took fire.

The Alamo was a necropolis: mangled, dismembered bodies, blood, and smoke. The never-ending wave of expendable Mexican soldiers trampled the corpses. They raided each chamber of the Alamo until everyone had been executed; and, finally, they discovered an indescribably beautiful blonde woman, a pretty little girl, and a little black boy secreted beneath a white tarp, behind a brace of hogsheads.

The woman, Susanna Dickinson, played by the actor Joan O'Brien, had been the wife of Captain Almaron Dickinson, killed at the Alamo. The little girl, Angelina Dickinson, named Lisa in the movie, and portrayed by John Wayne's daughter, Aissa, had been the Dickinsons' daughter, though an infant in 1836, not the girl of five or six portrayed by Aissa. One day, the real Angelina would become a prostitute; but that fact was a long way off, and she had no idea that the torment she bore that bright, bloody March 6 in 1836 would stretch on unrelieved until she died in agony at age 34. The little black boy might have been Colonel Travis's slave, Joe, who had also survived the massacre, but Joe had been 21 at the time, not a little boy.

In the final scene of the movie, Susanna hoisted her half-orphaned daughter onto a sad, white-muzzled donkey, led by the little black boy, maybe Joe, and paced alongside it among the carnage, through a phalanx of reverent Mexican troops at attention, as well the dashing, imperious Santa Anna, astride a pure white mount. As Susanna passed a Mexican peasant woman, the woman – as if she'd just beheld the apparition of the Virgin Mary – made the Sign of the Cross and bowed her head. My mother removed her hands from her face and made the Sign of the Cross, too.

Santa Anna removed his plumed hat and theatrically swept it in tribute to Susanna. She was maddeningly gorgeous, even erotic – her tailored pink frock, its frilly bodice, an alabaster floor-length apron. Ramrod-straight, defiant, her makeup flawless, a burnished smudge of filth on her camera-facing cheek that rendered her all the more fetchingly tragic, tendrils of flaxen hair wafting elegiacally from her French braid. A choir of seraphim had broken into "The Tennessee Babe," then imperceptibly transitioned into "The Ballad of the Alamo."

For three searing beats, Susanna halted and fixed the Generalissimo with what my mother called *the eyes* – her curse – then strode chastely by him – he was dead to her – and quite literally disappeared over a rise and into a firmament streaked with scarves of angels; and, as *THE END* bolted stoically across the screen like temple columns, the line "lie asleep in the arms of the Lord" was reprised by the choir.

The last image we glimpsed was that cockeyed cross over the ruined mission.

On the street, people hustled to get home before dark. It had rained and grown cold. My dad lit two cigarettes and handed one to my mother. She held my hand again. Steam rose from the sidewalk.

"Let's get some ice cream at Isaly's," said my father.

We jaywalked across Penn Avenue. My mother stopped in the middle of it, as a car, horn blaring, bore down on us. My father grabbed her and me and guided us through the traffic.

Under Isaly's awning sat a man with no legs on a platform attached to roller skates. It started raining again. Flurries floated down with it. Instead of begging, he rolled himself away with his hands along the sidewalk. Pigeons scurried ahead of him, dipping to scavenge filth riding the rain runoff in the gutter.

Isaly's was crowded. We grabbed the last unoccupied booth. My dad slipped off his coat, then helped me out of mine. An old woman in a green-and-white-checked uniform and a tiny crown-like paper hat, fastened with bobby pins, waited on us. Her brittle hair was dyed blonde, like my mother's. A paste of beige foundation on her face glared under the high-ceilinged fluorescent lights, orange eyebrows penciled above her lids. My father and I ordered grilled cheese and chocolate milk shakes. My mother hated milkshakes. She ordered a strawberry sundae. The waitress wrote our orders on a pad, placed an ashtray on the table, and called us *honey* and *dear*.

My mother asked her how she was.

"Tired," she replied, but she smiled. She asked me how old I was. I was six – in first grade – but I held up five fingers. I didn't want to speak. At the time, I thought my mother worked as a waitress. I wanted her to be as pretty as Susanna Dickinson –though the archival photographs of Susanna Dickinson, who would marry an additional four times after widowed at the Alamo, portray her as haggard and matronly, nothing at all like the exquisite Joan O'Brien.

The waitress moved along the counter, looking after her other customers. Every few minutes, she dipped beneath it for her burning cigarette and took a drag. She delivered our food and the check. The rain had given over to snow.

Alone on her side of the booth, my mother, still in her red coat, gazed past my father and me through Isaly's massive front window where the snow fell and streetcars whistled by. A bright red dab of strawberry clung to her lower lip. She was in the grip of whatever sometimes took her over, working herself up to something. To no one in particular, she asked, "Why did John Wayne have to die?"

My father reached across the table with his napkin, delicately dabbed away that bit of strawberry from her mouth, and said, "I don't know, Rita" – certainly to humor her, certainly because he wanted to avoid getting snarled up in an absurd conversation – or even an argument, a scene – in which he had to convince my mother that John Wayne – the living man, the actor – hadn't died. But, rather, the historical character, Davy Crockett, whom John Wayne portrayed in a movie rendition of history, had died – slain with his comrades at the Alamo 124 years ago. John Wayne was alive and well, likely in Hollywood, drinking beer or something manlier, smoking a cigar and enjoying the profits from *The Alamo,* his directorial debut (in which he had strangely chosen to murder himself) – not at all obsessing over us, as we sat in a dairy in an Italian neighborhood in Pittsburgh, as the snow picked up and night came on.

But, of course, my mother understood this. This was about something else – the cruel world, and all that it had taken from her. She had lapsed into that other realm – of the dead – that she sometimes inhabited; she was no longer with us.

My mother smiled at my father, as if in gratitude, then smiled at me – so memorably, as beautiful as any woman – and seemed placated, even happy. She dipped into her sundae and took another bite. Then she abruptly stood and walked by us.

"Rita," my father said, turned in the booth, and said her name twice more, not loud, but by then she was through the door, into the snow, and disappeared at the edge of Isaly's window.

For a moment, my father simply sat there, then he rose and wrangled me into my jacket, clamped my hat on my head, grabbed my hand and we ran for the door.

The old waitress yelled "Hey," and came around from the back of the counter, as everyone stopped and watched. Isaly's was a place where nothing bad could happen.

We paused for a moment on the sidewalk and peered into the snow coming fast now and coating the sidewalk. Among the throng pushing along Penn Avenue, through clouds of snow, bled my mother's red coat. Then she took the right on Highland. My father didn't yell, but called "Rita" – to himself, to me. She was much too far away to hear him above the roar along the avenue: trollies and cars, winter sweeping in on what had been a placid sunny day. It was almost too dark to see.

The waitress, brandishing our check, had followed us onto the sidewalk. "Come back and pay for this," she screamed. "You thieves. You lousy thieves."

My father picked me up and ran after my mother,

his breath chuffing out in white puffs. I wrapped my arms around his neck. The waitress, still screaming, and waving the check, toddled after us, then slipped on the icy concrete and took a bad fall.

My father turned on Highland and stopped for a moment to scan the avenue. Snow drilled his face. I turned away from it and looked over his shoulder. The sidewalk crowds had thinned. Merchants locked their doors and doused lights. The beggars burrowed into their rags. My father peered north into the dense white veil. As he stood there, winded, his breath a stream of fog, he shivered from the cold. He had left his coat in Isaly's. We spied a splotch of red. "Rita," he yelled and resumed his jog. By the time we made it to Hoeveler Street, we were the only ones out, apart from the cars and trollies, sorrowfully inching along. Even Foxx's Grille and Vento's Pizza had closed shop. Within the streetlamp haloes, snow convulsed.

Sirens wailed. Then, in the distance, flared a great red gash – smaller and smaller, gliding away from us – an ambulance hurtling over the Hoeveler Street Bridge – a kaleidoscope of crimson strobing the bloody flume of snow until it disappeared and even its siren faded, and we were shrouded in utter frigid silence. My father, shaking uncontrollably, stopped again. He gently set me down, then he sat in the snow on the sidewalk.

I had been about to cry when John Wayne died, but I held it in. I hadn't known that you can hold it in.

⁂

My Only Crack at Beauty

Colleen admits me through the Sterns' patio door. We kiss a long time. She smells of chlorine. She and Jonathan have been in the pool. He's already down for the night.

I love my visits to the Sterns'. Colleen and I play with Jonathan – eleven months old, cute, content, cooperative, beginning to toddle and babble. Then Colleen and I alone in this exquisite house – all glass and mirrors, white carpet, high ceilings, dangling chrome lamps, paintings that cover entire walls, a foyer bigger than my backyard on Saint Marie Street, bathrooms like spaceships.

Colleen and I eventually migrate upstairs to the Sterns' bedroom. We lie on their plush white bedspread and drink their vodka and orange juice out of monogrammed cocktail glasses. The late summer sun dwindles across us.

One of the glasses falls from the nightstand and breaks. Colleen does her best to clean up what's left of the screwdriver, but it's white carpet. I throw the towel and the broken glass in the bathroom trash. Colleen cries. I put my arm around her. That's when the Sterns, home much earlier than expected, walk through their big front door. They've insisted Colleen have the run of the house while she babysits Jonathan, but made a point when they hired her: *No boys on the premises.*

We hurry down the winding plexiglass staircase into the foyer. Right away, the Sterns notice Colleen's been crying and, of course, they don't know me.

Mr. Stern is handsome and beautifully dressed. I'm ashamed to be meeting him like this. He stretches out a hand. "I'm Macey Stern."

I take his hand. "I'm Fritz Sweeney."

"Fritz is my friend," says Colleen. She stands beside me.

"This is my wife, Melissa," says Mr. Stern.

Mrs. Stern is tall, dressed in black, one hand on her hip – long brown hair, dark eyes, a silver bracelet.

"How do you do, Mrs. Stern?"

She too shakes my hand, and says, "Hello, Fritz." Then, zeroing in on Colleen: "Is Jonathan alright?"

Jonathan has been fast asleep in his crib upstairs, but he suddenly begins to cry. Mrs. Stern races by us for the stairs.

Colleen clasps her hands together, her fingernails bitten red. She wears green and yellow-striped bell bottoms, low on her hips. Her blond hair is thick and long, all over her face and down her back; big, wet eyes ultramarine. She's trying not to cry, fretting her hands. She is fourteen years old – a sweet, anxious, fantastically beautiful girl I can't live without. My only crack at beauty.

Mrs. Stern returns, holding Jonathan. He's happy, clutching his mother's dress. Colleen hugs him, but he isn't friendly. He looks like his father. Colleen kisses Jonathan and tells him she loves him. I pat him and say, "See you, Buddy." He's got it made. He'll inherit all this.

Mr. Stern peels off bills from a money clip and hands them to Colleen. She thanks him lavishly. He smiles and holds out a hundred-dollar bill to me – I've never seen one before – ten times what he's just given Colleen.

Mrs. Stern looks at her husband, like *What the hell are you doing?* Colleen is, perhaps, too distraught to notice or doesn't find anything fishy about this.

I'm not clear on what this is all about. Maybe it's a set-up, some kind of sucker-game, a test. Maybe the hundred is a bribe, hush money, to prevent me from divulging something. But what? Maybe Mr. Stern is just being generous. Maybe I'm a peasant, and he's used to buying peasants: *I never want to see your sorry ass again.*

But what is Colleen? Not a peasant. Her father, like Macey Stern, is an attorney. Colleen scored this babysitting job because the Sterns and her parents are friends. They live in the same exclusive block.

My parents work for tips. I don't know how long it takes them to make a hundred bucks. I grew up around guys who would break Mr. Stern's jaw for insulting them with money – even though they covet all he has. My dad isn't one of them, but I wonder what he'd do in my place. My mother would tell Mr. Stern to shove goofy-looking Ben Franklin up his ass.

I'll never see Mr. Stern and his wife and baby again. I'll never set foot in their home again – nor will Colleen, as least not as their babysitter. The worry is that the Sterns will call Colleen's parents, whom I've never met. They don't even know about me. Colleen and I are brand new. We have a future together. It will be the end of us if the Sterns call, the end of Colleen. The Sterns are sure to discover we've dipped into their booze. And there's the towel and broken glass, the mussed bed.

Colleen says she'd love to sit for Jonathan again some time.

Things seem amiable enough. We say goodbye to the Sterns. Melissa Stern – swaying Jonathan to sleep on her shoulder and rubbing his back – smiles for the first time, though she nervously glances at that C-note her husband dangles in front of me, while Colleen, about to break down, remains oblivious.

Mr. Stern has never stopped smiling. It might be a smirk. *Take it or don't take it, you worthless fucking peasant. Whatever you do, it's your funeral.*

Rita's Dream

My mother had a dream about her father, Federico Schiaretta, immolated in the suspect fire, well before my birth, that destroyed his Station Street cobbler's shop. It was custom, almost liturgical, among Italians in East Liberty to summon a bookie and play a number, often a birth date, some scrap commemorating the beloved, any time they dreamt of a deceased relative.

My father, Travis Sweeney, did not seem at all a connected guy – an impression he deliberately fostered. Like my mother, he had grown up in East Liberty and knew plenty of mugs who took action. In fact, he knew everyone and about everyone, and preferred a kind of underground anonymity that was not so much cultivated, but inevitable. Yet my mother, Rita Schiaretta – on the surface, not his type at all – had seen through what others were unable to penetrate, and it was to him that she appealed the morning after the dream when she showed up at Foxx's Grille where he tended bar.

She worked next door to the bar as a receptionist in a dentist's office, a square, one-story, white block pillbox, with a golden name launched across the lone rectangular window facing Highland Avenue: *Sheldon Roth, Dentist.* Shelly Roth: a slick Jewish guy, educated and allusive, generous, chrismed and dandy, unapologetically friendly and effeminate. On the job, he wore a white tunic, but with panache. It buttoned up the side and fastened high on his neck. Like he was a baron or shaman or an ambassador from another planet. The neighborhood leagued him with the rackets. Some said he was dangerous. My father said the only thing dangerous about Shelly was his mind.

My mother was twenty-three, a graduate of Peabody High School, the dancer Gene Kelly's alma mater, where she had been a swimmer and student of promise, a young woman of wit and resource, certain to make her mark. Yet she had never made it out of the neighborhood.

There were things about herself she'd never know; and, on that day, December 23, 1953, ten o'clock in the morning, when she stormed into Foxx's expressly to request Travis Sweeney, a few years older than she, play a number based on a dream a mere six hours old, she would never have said that she had been cheated in the womb or that her attachment to vendetta was pathological. She did not realize these things about herself, nor would she ever, though all her life they would at every turn devil her and those she loved.

That day, my mother was neither bitter nor filled with inexplicable fury. It was before she started dyeing her hair, when her smile still had promise, and the things that would by and by become monstrous in her were innocent, sweet, even beautiful. When she was still committed to happiness rather than misery. Before her longing gouged a ditch through her heart.

She wore a plaid jumper and a red car coat, red gloves with red balls and furze at the fringe, red scarf, and red tam – as if she had dressed in the blood of the Yule to more passionately importune Travis Sweeney. Her eyes were brown and soft, a kindness imbedded in them. Her hands as well were soft. They would stay that way all her life, even as the rest of her hardened.

At the bar perched a string of played-out drummers in low-brim fedoras nursing shots and beers, stubbled gray faces pinched around filterless butts. They glanced up at her when she walked in. They knew her and her brothers. They knew her mother and how her father had died. She smiled fearlessly at them.

Foxx's was dark as a church. Mysterious spangles of light, through which dust nebula and reams of smoke wafted, hung like tinsel. The TV was on. *The Search for Tomorrow:* the stunted lust of the monochromatic early fifties. Christmas music: "Santa Baby," whined torchily by Eartha Kitt. Bing's "White Christmas." The Andrews Sisters: "All I Want for Christmas Is My Two Front Teeth." Next to the jukebox slouched a dwarfed artificial tree with a dozen pink bulbs and ropes of orange blinking lights that strafed the twinkling fifths queued behind the bar. A few sprung booths where people ate macaroni and ham and pickled eggs under a canopy of smoke. Neon beer signs: Straub, Duquesne, Iron City. A grease-splashed, framed, autographed glossy of Pirates slugger Ralph Kiner knitted at the corners with desiccated Easter palm.

Foxx's was the last flicker of my parents' childhood, the omniscient threshold of their futures. The final syllables of the prologue they'd been languishing in.

"Travis," my mother said, her voice mixing with the smoke.

"Hello, Rita."

"Will you do me a favor?"

"Anything."

"A cigarette."

My father smiled, slipped the scarlet package of Winstons out of his breast pocket, waved his hand over it like a magician, and proffered the pack with two cigarettes staggered out of its mouth like a TV ad. He wore a white shirt and pleated grey trousers. He possessed the cobalt blue eyes of a Siamese cat, a full head of furious black hair and a passionately pacific temperament. He liked to hang out with Black guys in the Hill District and listen to jazz at the Crawford Grill.

My mother chose the taller of the two cigarettes. My father flicked open a silver Zippo and spun the flywheel over flint. My mother, the beautiful white cigarette between her bloody red-lipsticked lips, leaned into the blue flame and took a puff.

"I want you to play a number for me." She smiled. "Please?"

"I thought the cigarette was the favor."

"It is, but not the one I came in here for. Can you play a number for me?"

"That's illegal, Rita."

"I won't tell anyone."

"I'd do almost anything for you, Rita."

"What wouldn't you do for me?"

"What I wouldn't do is ever tell you no."

"Then you'll do it?"

"What's the number?"

She had been awakened in the middle of the night by the unmistakable sound of her father's soft, almost womanly, voice, though he had been a man of singular hardness. Calling her name. Not Rita, but her christened name: *Carita.* Which means beloved, a derivative as well of the Latinate for charity: *caritas.* A dream, but not really a dream. A vision.

"You think I'm kidding?" my mother asked when my dad smiled bemusedly at her – and saw that flash, that slight declension, the rev behind her brown eyes that he would grow so acquainted with in the years to come. He was falling for her, yet he knew that she spelled trouble. He was a scholar of trouble. Loving Rita Sweeney would be his tragic flaw.

"No, I'm listening," he said. "A vision."

"Don't make fun of me, Travis."

"I'm not."

"I'll walk out of here."

"Please, Rita, continue. I'm not making fun."

At the sound of her name from her father's seared mouth, she had bolted upright in her single bed on Omega Street – the house she grew up in. She was surrounded by flames, as if the room itself was on fire – though no heat. In fact, the room had turned inexplicably cold. The white porcelain doorknob turned until released, and there in its naked jamb, wearing a suit of smoke, stood my dead cobbler grandfather. My namesake. He walked, lock-jawed, hands hidden at his back, to her bedside. Behind him burlesqued an entourage of smoldering souls, the convicts of Purgatory, writhing in a hurdy-gurdy of agony.

Smoke leaked from my grandfather's closed mouth, from his nostrils, his ears. When he removed his grey fedora, a tiny bow on one side of its maroon band, plumes of it flared toward the ceiling. He looked down upon his daughter, Carita, frozen to her little bed, its headboard draped with the rosaries her mother insisted upon, then above it the crucifix. The entire room a reliquary of statues and icons, her dresser and nightstand baroque altars of idolatry. A sick box on one wall; a holy water font affixed to another.

"I couldn't move," she told my father.

My grandfather had held out his hat. In it flared a nest of glowing red coals. He stirred them with a bare hand. His gray face grinded open.

"I have no memory of my father speaking to me. My whole life, I can't remember a word passed between us. And finally, he's speaking to me. I tried to rise to the sound of his voice, but I couldn't move, and I couldn't figure out what he was saying. Something in Italian. I just couldn't make it out."

Then Ouma, my exotically beautiful gypsy grandmother, given to wearing her dead husband's clothing – who traipsed between the worlds of the living and the dead, who guarded the portal against the dead – burst into the room. My mother could not be sure if Ouma was of the dream or if, indeed, she had been there in the flesh. Smoke lifted off Federico in white shrouds, like holy vapors from the thurible. But instead of frankincense came the stench of charred leather.

Ouma threw up the sash of the bedroom window. The night stormed in. My grandfather turned his back and walked out of the room. The poor souls of Purgatory followed him. My mother was sure she saw the Blessed Mother hovering above the flames they walked through – her blue mantle, the serpent curled about her ankle, the smile. The pact between her and her child, Rita Schiaretta.

"He was about to speak, Travis, to finally say something to me. Something that really mattered. I just know it. And then she opened that goddam window. I wanted to kill her, whether she was there or not." She took drag off the cigarette as my father stared at her. "I want you to play 311. March 11. His birthday. And his shop – the shop he died in – was 311 Station Street. Okay?"

My father obliged her with a wry smile that would become his signature for dealing with Rita Schiaretta. He didn't believe in those kinds of dreams or the prognostications Italians gave themselves over to in caprice or terror or sentiment. *Emozione*. He did not give credence to the numinous or fantastic. He did not believe in God. Though he understood better than anyone I've known that the mystical is often the tide of random, the inexorable erasure of history.

Nevertheless, he'd been mesmerized by Rita Schiaretta's wild tale – the mere fact that she had confided it to him. That she looked deeply into his eyes and clutched his forearm. He could tell that she was close to breaking down – that she was always close to breaking down – but she wouldn't have given him or those sons of bitches drooling at the bar the satisfaction. She'd walk out on Highland Avenue and fight any one of them. She'd rather take her place at the stake in Purgatory than let anyone see her shed a tear. He lit another cigarette and placed it in her mouth.

It was 1953 – not quite five months since the Korean War had ended. City Lights Bookstore had been founded in San Francisco by Lawrence Ferlinghetti and Peter Martin, something my dad knew all about, but had no one to talk it over with. McCarthy was ransacking America, galvanizing in young men like my father dreams of riding a motorcycle to California – though he knew he never would. He didn't even drive a car.

Smart as he was, and politically astute – he scoured daily the entire newspaper, had read books and studied history – and despite a practical streak of Black Irish blood, he had no ambition. By the time he and my mother struck their bargain, he was an agent of *ennui* and even knew the word; though, like so many words he reckoned the meaning of, not merely their definitions, he never uttered it. Nor did my mother possess a speck of ambition. It had all dwindled, then disappeared. But she had backbone, something she would accuse my father all their lives together of not possessing.

My father was already in love with Rita Schiaretta, though she'd swear for the rest of her life that she'd never thought twice about him until that day: two days before Christmas in the brutal Pittsburgh winter of 1953. My mother had already made her break with Ouma. By all accounts, she had taken her father Federico's death badly, though she despised him. Whatever might have really happened between my mother and grandmother, a woman I rarely saw, like all the stories moiling together in East Liberty, became irrelevant. A spate of nonspeaking became a lifetime of vendetta.

So: it was my mother who took her dream to Travis Sweeney, and Travis Sweeney who walked out Foxx's front door and hatched the deal with Philly Decker, a bookie who loafed outside the bar. Philly had then played the fin my mother had handed my father on my dead grandfather's birth date. And it came to pass, as foretold in lore, that the number hit on Christmas Eve for four hundred bucks, a small fortune, and my mother somehow convinced my father to trek with her to the Jersey shore for Christmas. Tales of similar magic are not uncommon in East Liberty.

My father hadn't wanted to go to New Jersey, but by this time he had his eye on my mother. Initially, he didn't say a word in response to her suggestion that they drive to the ocean in late December. The method he would come to adopt in coping with Rita Schiaretta was to humor her. He shot her a politely impassive look, as though he had his fingers crossed behind him. "Okay, Rita," he said pleasantly, not a trace of incredulity in his tone.

They left December 24, 1953, after their shifts had ended. Shelly Roth had insisted they take his '51 black Cadillac de Ville. He sure wasn't going anywhere for Christmas. As a little surprise, a bit of Christmas cheer, he had stashed a fifth of Four Roses on the front seat.

In that same red coat, gloves, scarf, the tam, my mother slid behind the wheel. My father, who would never learn to drive, something my mother never forgave him for, rode shotgun. He had a flashlight and a map. He illustrated for my mother the sagging crimson thread, the Pennsylvania Turnpike, that traversed the bottom of Pennsylvania, from Pittsburgh to Philadelphia. Pennsylvania was a near perfect rectangle, except for its jagged eastern border where it penetrated New York and New Jersey.

On the map, it was no larger than an open book of matches. The Atlantic Ocean, aqua blue at the map's edge, was mere inches from *Pittsburgh*, printed in big black capital letters. My mother had never seen the ocean – she had never been outside of Pittsburgh – and, because she could not bring herself to admit this to my father, acted as if she knew exactly where they were going. My father, who had not only seen the Atlantic, but the Pacific as well, sensed this about my mother, but it didn't matter – neither that she had never seen the ocean nor that she pretended she had. My mother was dangerous, my dad knew, bad news; but he couldn't turn away from her – as much fault his as hers.

He assured her that as her navigator he'd keep his eye on that red line on the map, that it would get shorter and shorter, as they traveled in the Caddy toward that immense pool of blue; and when the road was a nub, no more than a period at the end of a story, they'd smell the Atlantic. Then what could be better? She should check in with him every now and then along the way to see how close they were, to see if they were there yet.

No one had ever talked to my mother like this. That kind of hushed, unhurried inflection, the patience, that smooth, poetic way of putting things. She was a bit undone. My father's gentleness softened her resolve to tell all the world to go to hell. Yet she couldn't simply dismiss what he had to say as bullshit. Nor did she want to. Had there been anyone else around, she would have told my father off, told him to kiss her ass. But the two of them alone: what would it hurt for him to say such unimaginable things to her? It didn't seem to cost a thing.

A minute later, she asked, "Are we there yet, Travis?"

My father's finger, still on the line, moved slowly, as if of its own accord, like the planchette on a Ouija Board, as the de Ville rolled down Highland Avenue, through the heart of East Liberty, beneath the flashing Christmas bell garlands, on its way to the end of the earth.

My father laughed. She turned to him and smirked, an unlit Chesterfield in her mouth. He grabbed the cigarette and lit it, took a drag, then placed it back between her lips. Then he busted the seal on the Four Roses.

At this point, there's a gap in the story, a few missing pages. They easily could've hit bad weather and had to detour south, or they seized on a lark: Florida. Florida in 1953. Travis and Rita, 23 and 27, laughing, falling in love in Shelly's Caddy, drinking Four Roses, the bookmaker's four C-notes in Rita's purse, the snow repeating itself in white ceaseless shreds. Florida: because the ocean there, the same Atlantic that lapped gray and frigid against New Jersey, was warm as bathwater, amethyst blue. The sand was white. My father, in his vagabond days, had bathed in that warm blue water. Or they got lost. Or drunk.

They ended up in West Virginia – diffident and landlocked, shelved under Pennsylvania – crawling down a deserted dark winding road through a blizzard along the frozen Elk River. Florida's tepid, turquoise water was in another kingdom entirely.

"Are we there yet?" Rita asked.

"Not quite," answered my father. "But we're close. See that river." He pointed over at the ice-locked hoary Elk. "It runs into the ocean."

The snow dropped a white curtain over the Caddy. Blinded, it slid about the road. Massive bucks flanked the rimed shoulder, their racks silhouetted by the headlamps. Along the route out of Pennsylvania, and into West Virginia, the road had been littered with deer carcasses. Those bucks terrified my mother, their wanton abandon, their hobbled death wish.

Up ahead burned lights – the town of Darden. From utility poles on abandoned Main Street swung stars and tinsel. Not a soul on the street, but lights burned in all the silent houses lining it, and many of them had strips of colored lights framing their lintels and hanging from their eaves. My mother skidded into a parking lot, under a neon sign in busted-out purple cursive: *Elk Motor Court.* A string of blue Christmas lights swagged across the front of the motel. Next door was Crider's, a plywood store, spliced to a garage, no windows, with Esso pumps out front. On the other side of the river, smoke fumed out of the chimneys of little plank houses. Deer congregated on the bank.

It cost three dollars a night to stay at the Elk. Neither of my parents wanted to use real names, so they checked in as Mr. and Mrs. Charles O'Connor. The room was tiny. One bed with a baby blue chenille spread with a coin box, like those attached to the bucking plaster kiddie ponies outside the A&P. A dime made the bed vibrate. There was an unraveling fan-backed rattan chair. On the dresser, between a Bible and a green-faced alarm clock with white phosphorescent Roman numerals, sat a small black and white TV.

They left the room quickly and walked over to

Crider's. My mother could barely negotiate the frozen lot in her heels. Up on the mountain, a foot of snow had already fallen. It piled in the valley where they stood in the wind blowing off the brittle white river.

An old man with a long beard and galluses over a brown flannel shirt slumped behind Crider's counter. He wore an old-fashioned snap-brim like the aged Italian men who stood on the corner of Larimer Avenue and Meadow Street in East Liberty. In the middle of the concrete floor blazed a pot-bellied black wood stove and a pile of split black locust. Next to it was a large cardboard carton. The man asked them where they were from, where they were headed. My father explained that he and my mother were bound for the warm waters of Florida. My dad smiled at him and asked, "Are we close?"

The old man smiled back. "I reckon." His voice was gravelly, but the inflection was padded and slow.

There was rue in the eyes of those two smiling men, one very old and one very young. As if sharing a not entirely funny joke – that only they understood. As if they both knew, had always known, that my father and mother would never reach their destination. This old man: whose look my father recognized, who allowed in that look that he stood where he was behind that counter in Darden because he'd been thwarted himself, many years ago, in his original desire and destination. Not so much hard luck, but simply the way of it. He had taken his chance. We all choose. Just so. Not much to tell.

Because it was Christmas, because hope and illusion blazed so determinedly about them, the store man wanted to say to my father – whose mind, in turn, he was reading as well – that everything would be alright. Had he permitted himself to say it, maybe something would have opened up. Not just an opportunity for my mother and father, some windfall, some secret they'd discover, but even more than that – a hidden passage into another world, a staircase leading straight up through the roof and into the snowy mystery of the future. But the man hushed, and time stood still.

My mother stood next to the stove, holding open her red coat to its warmth, head flung back, eyes closed, long brown hair swinging out from her back. When she opened her eyes, the men were staring at her.

"Look in that box there," the old man said to her. He came out from around the counter.

In the box were six baby rabbits, each the size of a coffee cup. They were silvery brown with white blazes on their foreheads. Their eyes were tiny black pearls. They huddled together, twitching on a pink blanket spread on the floor of the box.

"Oh my God," my mother said.

"A dog killed the mama," said the man.

"What'll happen to them?" asked my mother.

"If they don't die, we'll raise them for the table."

"You'll eat them?"

"Yes, ma'am. If they don't die."

"May I have one?" My mother turned and looked at the man.

My father did not at all want a wild infant rabbit. It was an utterly absurd notion, no less absurd than borrowing Shelly Roth's Cadillac for a trip to New Jersey, then Florida, and getting stranded in a blizzard in some godforsaken mountain town in West Virginia – every bit of it predicated on a crazy dream my mother had had about her dead Italian shoemaker father. But the number had hit. There was something to that. My mother was about to turn and ask my father if they could adopt one of the rabbits. He knew that if he did not dig in right then and there, once and for all, and pronounce, "Hell, no, Rita, we're not carting that rabbit along with us," for the duration of his life on earth, he would be powerless against her.

He didn't want to lose her, but he didn't know why he wanted her so much or if he really wanted her at all. How could there be both? Wanting and not wanting? After not even half a day with her, she was already a habit – like dope or booze or cigarettes, things people fall in love with that destroy them. The old man was pinned down by my mother's gaze. Maybe, like my father, he had never really known what he wanted. But Rita Schiaretta always knew what she wanted and when she wanted it – even if it was anathema. And in that moment – just before the old man, said, "Yes, ma'am, pick you one out," and Rita, still holding to the very last minutes of her girlhood, turned to my father with her beautiful brown eyes and pretty smile – Travis Sweeney accepted my mother and the sacred vow of fatalism to which he'd remain forever steadfast. He smiled at her, and said, "Of course," before she opened her mouth.

She was bending into the box when the man added, "It'll be dead by morning."

Though my father knew this was true, he put his arm around my mother and the bunny she held in her arms and said, "Maybe not."

"We'll take care of him," said my mother.

"Yes, we will," my father added.

"You got to feed him with an eyedropper," said the man.

"We can do that. Can't we, Travis?"

"Absolutely."

The old man looked at my father. He understood every bit of what had transpired, and he wanted my father to know he knew. Not that he condemned my father for it. He would have done the same thing. It was wrong for my father to give his consent on the rabbit. Wrong for the old man to permit it in the first place. He held my father an instant longer in his stare. That little rabbit was going to die.

"Alright then," the man said. "I'll fix you up some formula." He disappeared through a door at the back of the store that led to a bay. A car was up on the lift and, under it, a man with a mask and a blowtorch. Sparks rained down on him.

My parents, the tiny rabbit in the crook of my mother's arm, walked along the dusty shelves. They bought cigarettes, a six-back of Tasmanian Lager, potato chips, a wedge of hoop cheese, bread, and chocolate milk.

When the man returned, he had a shoebox padded with rags and a mason jar half-filled with white liquid. He handed these to my father and then an eyedropper.

"You got to feed him every three hours. Just this. You give him anything else, you'll kill him. And don't give him too much."

"What's in it?" asked my mother.

"Little Karo syrup, sweet condensed milk, some egg yolk. It's to be warm when you give it to him. Remember. Nothing else, but what's in this. And keep that little thing warm. And feed him slow or you'll drown him."

"We'll pay for that," my dad offered.

"Well," said the man. "I'm not giving you much. He'll be dead in the morning."

They waited for him to say something else. He and my father shook hands.

"Thank you," said my mother. Then she hugged the man, who closed his eyes and held her a moment.

When he came away, he said, "Don't pet him. They can't take handling."

My mother and father turned with their groceries and the trembling rabbit, now held against my mother's breast, under her coat, and walked out of the store.

Across the road from Crider's was a church. In its front yard a crèche had been set up. Statues big as people. Cows and sheep, too. They were difficult to make out for the pounding snow, the blurred pointillism. The statues moved – imperceptibly. They were real people. Like a play. Out there in a blizzard. Joseph and Mary and the shepherds. Real animals. Angels with wings and haloes. Even a real little baby. In awe, Rita and Travis paused and stared.

"Where are the Wise Men?" my mother asked.

"They're lost," explained my dad. "They won't get here until January 6."

"We're not lost. Are we, Travis?"

"No, Rita, we're not lost. Not in any conventional sense."

"But we're not there yet, are we?"

"Maybe not quite, but close. For most people, close is pretty good."

"Let's stay here, Travis, and wait for the Wise Men."

At that moment, Christmas Eve, 1953, Travis Sweeney and Rita Schiaretta, independent of each other, contemplated stepping away from the destiny that awaited them in Pittsburgh, and accepting the invitation of that poor, little one-horse town, ringed by the Appalachian Mountains they couldn't quite see for the snowstorm. Unknowingly, they had stumbled across one of the invisible portals that exist in the mysterious ether – those we walk blindly by day in and day out: the entry into another life in another place, the chance to be better, to be the someone we desperately wish to be, the someone we actually are, but don't realize. Through the scrim of snow, they had caught a blurred glimpse of that other life the old man at Crider's had been on the verge of telling them about.

I want to say that portal is not so otherworldly, not some *Twilight Zone*-like parallel universe. I want to say that the fare into that other world, the better world, is love, but for that kind of love – the love that chooses happiness over self-immolation – my mother, though she desperately wanted it, was ill-equipped. She simply could not locate the seam bordering love and suffering.

My father knew nothing about tending a crop or livestock, how to split wood, drive a tractor. He was not that kind of man. He was not physically resourceful. He rarely got dirty. But he was unafraid of the earth he stood on at any given moment, of what it hides and might render. He was about to tell Rita this – in those very words since he realized that something was happening between them, that on that evening carefully wrought words mattered very much to her, that no one had ever talked to her the way he had – or at least gotten away with it. If he chose his words with precision and passion – *I am unafraid of what the earth hides and might render* – she would be his.

My mother saw in that little hamlet mantled in white a confounding, ineffable beauty for which she had no language. She thought about living there. But do what? She would have babies. She would dip her hands into the earth. She would plant a life there in Darden. Shriven of her father's assassination by fire, her gypsy *strega* mother. The vendetta and recriminations. She could stop being Italian. And become Travis Sweeney's.

Gazing down slumbering, snow-shrouded Main Street in Darden, West Virginia – a place that may not have even existed – the very Nativity itself hatching before her very eyes, she felt that perhaps this was her entrance into the dark heart about to explode in light. Then she pictured Shelly. Would he laugh at her? "You're too smart for that, Rita. You can be somebody. What the hell are you going to do down there?"

And these people? They were good people – in this little town. My mother could tell from the lights in their houses. Busting their asses trying to figure it out. No different from the Napolitano East Liberty peasants she issued from.

Shelly was a queer Jew dentist living above his shop on Highland Avenue. Plenty of nights he ended up in Foxx's, then later upstairs suffering. He knew the score. He might sit down and pull out a cigarette from his white tunic. Take both her hands. "Get out of East Liberty, Rita. Nothing's ever going to happen again here. You've got that script memorized. You and Travis. You're brilliant. You're beautiful." Shelly would laugh. "Move to West Virginia. Buy a farm. You're only young once. Take a chance."

But the country – the streams and fields, the sound of beasts in the woods, the dizzying vertigo of this altitude. Everything unchecked, unpaved, unbeholden. She'd grow angular, her mouth a hyphen, hair like dried black thistle. A thin faded blue dress with tiny yellow flowers on it. Eyes out on her cheeks – a tetched Appalachian Napolitana. The land terrified her. She wanted high heels, to ride the streetcar downtown to Gimbel's, go to the show. There probably wasn't even a hospital or A&P. Why not just take the banana boat back to Naples?

My father had been watching her, mesmerized. The blood red coat and high heels in a blizzard, cradling that baby rabbit against her, a powerful twenty-three-year-old girl skating along the blade of a razor. The cryptic Appalachian range peered far into the future, beyond Travis and Rita and me, their only child, beyond my progeny's progeny and even beyond the point where everything is forgotten.

My father had already learned to read my mother's mind, a fabulous talent, but one that would aid him little over the years in predicting what she might do. He had fallen for her, for her wild, unbridled fear of earth: fear that would claw her hands through her long wavy brown hair – before she began to dye it blonde, against my father's wishes – and pour invective like lighter fluid from her red-lipsticked mouth; and, often worse, suture in silence that same mouth for days, weeks – not even to eat, barely to breathe. Because her great power, her insupportable curse, was wielding silence like one might wield a blade or revolver.

But they were still locked in that little vial of magic. It was in my father's power to alter their course, to swerve out of the oncoming – with just a word. But which word? My mother was afraid. That's what it was, what it had always been. If my father would have said something, she would have followed him. That Christmas Eve in Darden, she would have followed him anywhere. But he had to say it. He had to have the backbone to say it.

When they got back to the The Elk, they wrapped the rabbit in towels and placed it on the bed. It lay peacefully on its side, its flank caving with each gentle suspiration. My mother rubbed its ears and ran her fingers across its plush fur. The smoke from my parents' cigarettes shone in the rabbit's black oracular eyes.

"Rita, honey, you should try not to pet him too much."

"I know, I know, but he's such a baby."

"He is. He's dear."

"You're dear, Travis. The things you let yourself say are dear." She laid her hand on my father's. He looked down at their hands, locked on the blue spread.

"Rita," my father said.

She smiled. "Tonight is more than anything I've ever had. It's like a dream."

My dad brought my mother's beautiful hand to his lips and kissed it. "We should feed this bunny," he said.

They warmed an eyedropper of formula with a Zippo. Rita placed the drowsy rabbit in her lap and fed it. It took the food slowly, deliberately. Little clicking noises as it sucked and swallowed. Two droppers.

"He's hungry. He wants more," Rita said.

"The gentleman at the store said don't overdo it."

"You think he's okay? He's going to be okay. Isn't he, Travis?"

"I think he'll be fine. We'll follow instructions to the T. He'll be fine." It was 10 o'clock. My dad got up and set the alarm clock for 1 a.m. "But you should try not to pet him, Rita."

My mother fondled the rabbit, now asleep in her arms. "That's it," she vowed. "I'm going to stop now. Poor little lamb." She set the rabbit, wrapped in the towel, next to her on the bed, then patted the bed for my father. He lay down, the rabbit between them, and turned off the lamp. A blue swaying luster from the blowing Christmas lights beyond their window fell across the three of them. In a six-foot drift, Shelly's lone black Caddy brooded in the The Elk's lot. Coyotes yammered from the ridge, but my parents mistook them for the yowling wind. They lay in silence, smoking cigarettes, for a long time.

Suddenly, my mother stood. "I'm going to get him settled. I'm afraid we'll suffocate him." She picked up the sleeping rabbit, cuddled it against her face, kissed it, swaddled it up again in its towel, tucked it back into its shoebox, walked a few steps to the dresser and set it down. She switched on the TV and dialed through the fitful stormy channels. "Maybe there's something Christmassy."

By the light of the TV, my dad spread the food from Crider's on the bed. "Are you hungry, Rita?"

"I think I am." Then: "This is all that's coming in clear." *Bird of Paradise,* with Louis Jourdan and Debra Paget. "Will he be warm enough, Travis?"

"He's going to be fine. We can put him on top of the TV once it heats up."

My mother flopped on the bed. My parents drank whiskey from the motel's cloudy plastic cups and the bitter beer straight from its blue cans. They ate the cheese and bread and potato chips. They drank the chocolate milk.

My dad whipped out a dime and dropped it in the slot. The bed groaned and twisted, shuddering like a cold car trying to turn over. My mother couldn't even get her cigarette lit.

"You're an ass, Travis," she said, laughing.

The movie was tragic. A Frenchman (the dashing Jourdan) visits his high-born Polynesian college roommate's island paradise, falls in love with the roommate's exotic, impossibly exquisite sister (Paget), marries her and remains on the island.

My mother plucked tissues from The Elk's magenta Kleenex box. The gorgeous islands, the jungle birds soaring in the cloudless sky, the warm soft sparkling ocean reminded my parents that they were bound for the Atlantic. In both of them, simultaneously, grew a longing, the gnawing for peace and goodness. There would never be quite a moment like this again between them. They, of course, had not known this then, nor should they have. There had been too much augury already in their bargain. But they did know the little they knew – it could have only been love – and that was enough to keep them together – God Help them – for the rest of their lives.

The bed shuddered to a halt. My father leaned over and kissed my mother, gently and with honor. Their first kiss. My mother was a woman to stick a knife in a man she couldn't suffer kissing her. My father kissed her again – with more ardor and intention. She knew then – as if in possession of the future, a talent passed on to her in blood by her mother – that she would never meet a more memorable man than Travis Sweeney.

She wore a pretty silver satiny blouse, and she began to unbutton and move out of it. It was clear, from the way she looked at my father, the cast of her depthless brown eyes, that this was part of the ritual, that he should in no way interfere. He sat and watched, realizing that the machinery of something completely unpredictable, but inevitable, had been set in motion.

She opened the blouse and lifted it upward off her shoulders, down her arms, behind her and held it spread open that way, like wings, for a moment. Her brown hair was long. She looked at my father who sat before her, mesmerized. She was his angel, neither good nor a bad angel, but merely a fallen confused one, like himself; and he almost interrupted her, halted her kermis, as if to go back in time, because more than anything, he was flooded with the certain knowledge that she would reveal to him terrible things. Had he dropped his eyes, or closed them, diverted his attention in the slightest, my mother would have retracted her wings, covered herself, pinned back her hair, and walked out into the blizzard.

My father did not even permit himself to blink or breathe. This moment had been foretold, somewhere in the writ, and there was no turning back. She folded the blouse and laid it across one of the arms of the chair. Then she wiggled out of her skirt, bending her knees slightly, and twisting back and forth in a shimmy till it fell. She laid the skirt across the other chair arm and, with her back to my father, removed the rest of her clothing and dropped it in the lap of the chair.

Then she stilled, in the lamplight, fully illuminated. Her hair fell to her shoulder blades, then the long drop of her unmarked body – like a famous painting of a nude, maybe Renoir: that composed incandescent quality of an untouchable dream woman, a conjured woman, immured in paint on canvas and framed, though no less real for one's longing for her. Perhaps it was the cast of gauzy light, from the lamp and television, where the taboo love between the Frenchman and the Polynesian had become clearly doomed, the plot lurching deeper and deeper into the darkness.

My mother was preparing to turn and face my father: to reveal whatever he had been summoned to this hidden patch in a mountain blizzard to reckon, and the unimaginable chain of events her turning would trigger. He had signed on for it. It was no longer his to halt. He'd not be spared the agonizing secrets of love: not merely what had been waiting so devoutly beneath her clothes, but the devastating tumult of her blood, and the vengeance meted out by it. Such rectitude was a long way off, yet my father sensed it marshaling in her, like a freak blizzard lurking in a placid sky. There was nothing he could do to prevent it.

So he laid back against the headboard, swigged another ounce of Four Roses, lit a cigarette, just as my mother turned to face him, allowing him to study her in the light for just an instant – the various intersections of her limbs and torso, the nuanced hollows, what she refused to cover, her arms at her sides, hands open mid-thigh, as if daring him to look away, as if testing him – before she extinguished the light of the lamp, as if lowering the curtain, on the last recorded second of Carita Schiaretta's girlhood – Travis Sweeney, like a documentarian, there to record the moment.

She remained at the foot of the bed, now bathed in the holographic sepia convulsions of the television, and the watery purple light from the Elk Motor Court neon. Then she climbed onto the bed, snugged against my father like a second skin, and kissed him deeply, with intent and alarming might. He wished desperately to open a window, at least gaze through it and assure himself of the frozen world.

Suddenly my mother sat up, perched cross-legged before him, clutched a corner of the blue spread, and covered herself. Her face, the hair spangled over it, and her partially concealed breasts were lavender.

"I still want to go to Florida, Travis." She fetched her whiskey.

"We'll set out again tomorrow."

"You promise?"

"Yes, I do, Rita. For now, let's drink to your old man, the philanthropist who funded this adventure."

"To Papa Fred," said my mother, raising her plastic cup. "The only decent thing he ever did."

For a moment, before they drank, before they turned down the bedclothes, my grandfather, Federico, in one of the expensively tailored suits he somehow sported on cobbler's wages, smoldered in front of them. He had crossed the ocean, Italy to America, that they might share this fateful night together in a Braxton County, West Virginia, blizzard: his daughter, Carita, and a dreamy Black Irishman who aspired to nothing loftier than to be left to his thoughts.

When a deadly volcano erupted, Debra Paget, too

beautiful to live, flung herself to appease the gods into its spewing mouth. My mother jumped up and snapped off the TV, reached into the shoebox, stroked the rabbit for a moment, and bundled it up again. Then she crumpled on the bed and wept. My dad pulled her to him, popped another dime into the box, and the two of them – not quite there, but closer every moment – resumed their journey to the Atlantic.

Some time, during the long holy night, as the snow prognosticated, my mother rose, and placed back in bed between her and my father the slumbering rabbit.

⁎

About the Author

Joseph Bathanti is the former North Carolina Poet Laureate (2012-14) and recipient of the North Carolina Award (for Literature), the state's highest civilian honor. He is the author of twenty books, including poetry, fiction, and nonfiction, and has co-edited volumes of poetry. Bathanti is Professor of English and McFarlane Family Distinguished Professor of Interdisciplinary Education & Writer-in-Residence of Appalachian State University's Watauga Residential College in Boone, North Carolina. He also teaches in Carlow University's low-residency MFA Program in Creative Writing in Pittsburgh, the city in which he was born and raised. He served as the 2016 Charles George VA Medical Center Writer-in-Residence in Asheville, North Carolina, and is co-founder of the Medical Center's Creative Writing Program.

CPSIA information can be obtained
at www.ICGtesting.com
Printed in the USA
LVHW100300240723
753120LV00004B/290

9 781958 094273